BIRDWILD

BIRDWILD

written by
Bobbi J. Simmons

The BlackGold Publishing Book League

Published by BlackGold Publishing
Edited by: N. Brooks, D. Jenkins, A. Hernandez

1706 Todds Lane, Suite 258
Hampton, VA 23666

TABLE OF CONTENTS

Dedicated to the loving memory of my personal
guardian angel in heaven that watches over me:

**God created mothers as special as can be
But he made one extra-special
And gave her to me.**

(Louise Williams-Crawford 3.12.35)

GOOD-BYE

The summer of 1968 ended and the Breeze family's brand-spanking new house was finished and ready for them to move into. The move was very bittersweet for Bree because of the peace she felt in the smaller house that sat in the middle of open land with very few trees. The only visible trees were those that sat in the back yard over the chicken coops and near the entrance to the fenced garden. In the center of the small pig pen sat an old Oak tree with branches that extended beyond the reaches of the wire and poles used to have confined livestock. She internalized so many feelings of displacement and abandonment from the place she had loved for the past ten years.

Bree looked helplessly from side to side and from the front to the back of the car's windows to have gotten one last panoramic view of the little house that sat in the middle of miles of open field. Feelings of panic spread into the core of her stomach. Bree felt sad, weird, and almost manic. Tears welled up but never fell. They rode the ten miles while Daddy shared versions of all his greatness with them. Where he had been and where he was.

The family had driven the ten-mile trip once a week to view the building progress. She knew this time would be different. They arrived and Daddy parked at the back entrance of the house. Bree and the family entered at the rear of the house and saw the picturesque patio near the pond that displayed statues of lions on columns. Plants had been planted around the water fountain, as well as rows of Palm trees that extended to the pond.

"Wow, this looks like a picture out of a book or a movie."

"I saw a picture that looked like that."

"That is so pretty."

"Wow! I like those flowers," Bree spoke uncontrollably.

"Yeah, it does look good, don't it? Those fellows did a good job on the garden," Daddy said to the family.

All their voices echoed throughout the entire bottom level of the house when they took turns and described what they saw. The view from the kitchen reminded Bree so much of an old southern movie with a mansion that had its own cook. The rest of the house, other than the gardens, seemed cold, hard and fake. The enormous chairs and sofas in the formal living room were covered with thick plastic, surrounded by heavy dark designer curtains that hung across each of the many windows throughout the house.

After the excitement dissipated, the family went their separate ways to soak up the remainder of the house.

This would be another bittersweet moment for Bree. Because in the excitement of the move, it was also her birthday. But just like all her other birthdays, this one too was, overlooked and forgotten. She pushed pass her thoughts and ran out to the pond. From the banks of the pond turtles were seen as they sunbathed on broken limbs that had fallen from the nearby trees. And along the edge she could see small fish as they swam away. Birds chirped in the background as the wind carried their songs. Bree took in all the new surroundings the pond had to offer. She picked up a rock that laid at her feet. For a quick moment she remembered the scene from the Andy Griffit Show when Opie threw the rock on the small pond and it skipped across the water. Bree stood with the rock in her right hand. A quick squat and the rock sailed and skipped across the water three times.

"Wow!" Bree smiled. She searched for more rocks and continued to entertain herself with each skip. A high pitched voice startled her just as the rock left her hand.

"Bree, Bree come back up here," Mama said from the back porch of the house.

As the delight of the day ran its natural course. She had hoped the call was for a surprise birthday cake with candles she could huff and puff until smoke filled the air. Bree came inside and sat at the table in the kitchen, disappointed that she did not see any birthday surprises. Her spirit dropped and tears grew in her eyes again. The heavy hope for some form of a birthday wish or celebration was gone.

"Why don't they love me?" Bree's liveliness diminished into tears.

Her thoughts gave way to the times her friends had talked about their birthdays at school.

"Why does Sammy and Rachel, Cheryl and Michael and the others have birthday parties, and I don't?" She felt adrift.

"Go upstairs child and look at your new bedroom," Daddy snapped her back to where she was earlier.

The family got up from the kitchen table, and went their separate ways to have explored the rest of the house. Junior took off upstairs and raced Bree up the spiral stairs. They found their bedrooms that sat at opposite ends of the hallway. Bree rushed past the pink floral coverings on her queen-sized bed. Beyond the pink floral curtains that matched the bed spread was the luscious and inviting body of water she had just left. The scenic fairy tale world at the top end of the stairs was a picturesque contemplation of calm loneliness. She moved beyond her excitement and lowered her body onto the recliner at the foot of her bed.

Mama hung back in the kitchen, and basked in its sunny warm yellow colors. The energy seemed to have absorbed into her soul, and for a brief moment she was at peace. Until she caught a glimpse of the man of the hour as he strutted around like a Congo Peafowl Peacock. His chest stuck out, pompous, and arrogant with his head held high and completely drunken off the wine of himself.

"Berta, they did a good job, didn't they? All the mess I had to put up with, you know I had to make them redo that bathroom in the hall, and the rails on the stairs, they kept messing them up. But they are all done now, so glad they are through." His arrogance rose up like storm clouds, and the true narcissist he had become rushed out like a strike of lightening.

The grandest part of his persona was the self-importance he felt he had contributed to his world and the community of Allendale, South Carolina.

Bree and Junior sat at the top of the stairs and listened to their Daddy.

"Here we go," Bree rolled her eyes back into her head as Daddy started a conversation about himself.

Bree and Junior walked slowly to the kitchen. The family had assembled in the kitchen after visiting the rooms upstairs. Her Father was feeling higher than a kite in the sky when he started.

"So what do ya'll think?"

But before an answer had hit the air Daddy continued.

"I know; I know this house is something else. Yes, Lord they did a good job."

Bree looked at Junior and shook her head back and

9

forth. All Mama heard was, "Lord ya'll know it ain't easy being me."

"Hee, hee I know these nobodies around here are talking about me. That's what happens when you do something like this. But that's enough about me talking, about me. I'm going let yawl talk about me, hee, hee."

Bree, Junior and Mama rolled their eyes at the same time.

Bree wondered what store he had shopped at in order to have found a hat big enough to fit the whopping head that housed that huge ego of his.

She questioned why her Father felt he had to have proven so much of himself to the world. But for now, they pretended to have listened to his bodacious bragging.

"Why don't you just shut up, old man," Junior whispered to his sister.

In his heart, her Daddy and only him knew his words to be the truth. If not the truth it would be the story he would have stuck to no matter what.

At the tender age of thirty-eight, Wallace was somewhat of a pint-sized man with a complexion so dark and smooth that it shined when he stood in the brightness of the sunlight. A rounded face that stood out like the black patent leather shoes he so proudly wore to church services and even to the store. His appearance and what he wore, spoke with volumes of the extendedness of his ego.

The big wide-rimmed country cowboy hats that matched his pointed country cowboy boots (What black man wore cowboy hats and boots?). Not to mention those Fedora derbies he wore that meticulously matched his bold, colorful leisure and dressed suits and laced up wingtip shoes.

After the gathering in the kitchen for the brag session, Bree and Junior went back upstairs to their bedrooms. Daddy walked into the garden, and Mama remained seated at the kitchen table.

"Why are they all so uncaring? Why didn't anyone say happy birthday?" Bree sat at the foot of her brand-new bed and cried uncontrollably tears she had held back earlier. She wiped her tear-stained face and laid her lifeless body across the foot of the bed.

As she reached for one of the many pillows to rest her head for comfort, she stroked the pillows that were identical to the curtains and bedspread. Her hands were surprised when she stumbled upon a sudden hardness.

"What in the world is that?"

Mama had placed two white dolls underneath the pillows on the bed. A surprise she had hoped, would have somehow made Bree more girlish. For a very brief moment, she smiled inside and thought that just maybe, Mama had cared about her birthday.

But as she stared into the eyes of the miniature figures that reminded her of the few white girls she had seen at the store when she and Cousin Matthew rode their bikes to get their sweet candy and treats. Her mind reminisced about her favorite cousin, and how she wished he was there. She stroked the doll's long blond hair, caressed the pale white skin, skin hard and cold like the plastic coverings on the chairs in the formal living room.

She felt no connection, and threw the doll across the room.

"A white doll? Why would I want a white doll? "

"Nah, she makes me sick, what do I want with these fake white dolls?" The mood changed to one of anger.

"Is this what they see when they look through me?" Thoughts of how she looked lingered heavily in her mind. She thought about words her Mama and Daddy had said so often in anger about her looks.

The confines of all this pink prettiness utopia made it hard to believe that just outside the walls of this world was a world of family enigmas that shaped the boundaries of her life for the rest of her life.

COOL DAYS OF COUNTRY

"Sit still, child!" Mama shouted over and over because she was tensed and wound up tighter than the new clock that ticked away above the kitchen's sink. She smooth Bree's uninhibited scalp and edges with grease from the almost empty jar at the edge of the kitchen counter.

"Hold your ears gal and lean over so I can get to your kitchen and edges. Child, your head is a mess. It's going to take me a long time on your head. It'll be dark before I get done today," Mama said and rubbed the back of her hand across her sweaty forehead.

The heat from the stove was a mirrored image of the heat that stood strong outside. She was fidgety and moved around in the chair that had no cushions. Cushions she so very much needed to support her bottom and back.

Today her energy was high and practically out of control. Her tiny body jerked and twisted and turned when it should have been still. Matthew, her most favorite cousin in the whole wide world, had come from New York to visit for the summer. Matthew had been outside for the last hour or more and waited eagerly by the back door for his favorite cousin. His lack of patience caused him to make several unannounced visits to the backdoor. His restlessness led to a game of peek-a-boo on the porch from behind the screen on the door. While he fought off the pesky

13

flies and nats that swarmed around his head. Pesky pretty much like Mat was on the back porch.

"Why are you taking so long? Gosh, I'm tired of waiting out here in all this heat and these nasty nats," Matthew said as he walked back to the bottom of the steps. He could not for the life of himself understood why it took so long for his cousin to have made her debut in the backyard. Matthew thought his motions and movements of cunningness would have sped up his aunts' work. Bored with the game on the porch, Mat decided to go back to his uneventful day in the backyard.

"Go back out there in the yard and play, boy.

She'll be done when I get done.

Getting on that one last nerve I got left," Mama mumbled under her breath.

The weekly routine for her was not as bothersome when Cousin Matthew was not around. Today she sat at the table in the kitchen of their newfangled house on a late Saturday afternoon, and her blood boiled piping hot. A hotness like the grease Mama used to fry the catfish that laid in the sink, and waited to be gutted and cleaned.

"Child, if I tell you one more time to be still, God is going to need to help you and your stingy little soul," Mama said this time as she tried so hard not to cuss. The handle of the straightening comb on the stove had overheated because the heat of the stove was too high. "Dammit that hurt, burnt my hand, messing around with you and that boy out there." Mama blurted out so loud her voice traveled beyond the walls of the house and landed on the back porch. The hot comb hit the floor, and the entire kitchen went mute.

Matthew killed the silence when he ran full steam ahead into the back door. He had obviously forgotten about the screen he had just whispered through. He hit the door, toppled over and fell backwards onto the porch, causing a large crashing sound.

Bree and Mama were startled beyond the hotness of the straightening comb. They both without hesitation, ran around the opposite sides of the table to the backdoor.

"What in the world?

What have you done, boy?

Didn't you see that door?

Have you lost your mind?

Crazy as a bed bug." Mama pelted out one question after another to her collapsed nephew without waiting for his returned answers. Matthew lay sprawled out on the cemented slab, designed to create an entrance to the back door. Flat on his back, he looked like a wounded animal. Mama repeated her original statement this time as she stood directly over her nephew. Bree's face was full of anxiety and concern as she looked at her favorite cousin's pain riddled face. Matthew scrambled until he reached the railing on the porch and pulled himself to his feet. When Mama saw that he was okay, she turned and inspected what damage he had done to the door.

"You seem to be more concerned with the harm caused to the door than Matthew's head," Bree mumbled underneath her breath.

"Are you okay, Mat?

Come on. I'll help you to the chair." Bree helped him to his feet. She removed a cushion from a nearby chair and placed it by his head.

"Huh, running into that door like you don't have any sense. I know Maw Maw raised you better than that," the air stiffened with the foulness of her tone. With a quick turn, she sashayed back to the kitchen.

 "Get back in here gal so I can get done with your nappy head. I still need to gut and clean that fish in the sink. Lord knows that fish ain't gonna fry itself, or that cornbread mix itself and fly into that frying pan." The old wicked witch of the east had spoken her piece. Matthew followed Bree into the kitchen, grabbed a glass from the cabinet and filled it with water from the sink.

"What are you doing? These glasses are used at supper time, not when you just feel like grabbing one. From now on, you get water out there from that water hose. Coming in here, dirtying up these dishes like you are the one that wash them, do you hear me?

The old witch was still hissing.

"Yes, ma'am, I'm sorry." Mat looked at his aunt with pain still in his face.

"Are you all right?" Mama asked with an un-nurtured and flustered attitude.

"Yes, ma'am. I'm okay, Aunt Berta," Matthew said with kindness and a gentle smile. Maw Maw had done a great job with Matthew.

Once again, Mama stood at the back of Bree's chair while the straightening comb sizzled and popped from the hair grease that laid on the ends of her hair and near her scalp. Bree's body tensed every time the heat almost grazed her scalp. She felt Mama's apron when it brushed against her as she completed a straightened section of hair and moved it to the side. Her apron was tied tightly around her once slendered waist, and her rounded stomach made the imprinted roosters and hens with their baby chicks poke out in front of her. The stained apron reeked of the slimy catfish scent in the kitchen's sink that had stagnated the air along with the smell of Bree's burnt hair.

It was a smell that later turned to delight when the catfish and cornbread graced the supper table. The fried catfish and stovetop cornbread were a Saturday evening feast the family looked so forward to and gobbled every bite like it was their last supper.

Bree had been chewing on a piece of Bazooka Bubble Gum for the last hour. She entertained herself when she blew small bubbles and sucked them back in before Mama knew. The last bubble she blew was bigger than the ones she was used to, and was so impressed she forgot to suck it back in. It popped, and the sound covered the kitchen. All hell broke loose in the kitchen. Mama pitched a hissy fit for the next thirty minutes.

After ten minutes of her saying the same thing over and over, Bree's mind moved to thoughts of her and Cousin Matthew's bike ride to the old country store the day before when the heat of the day was less invasive. The old country convenience store sat alone on a dirt road away from the railroad tracks that ran the entire length of the Eastern Seaboard. A two-mile ride for the two at most when coming from the house. The bike ride generally took fifteen minutes when they cruised, but yesterday they raced against each other, so the time was cut in half.

"I won, I won again," Matthew stood by his cousin's bike and raised his hands in the air to have celebrated his victory.

"Yeah, yeah, whatever with them old long skinny legs," Bree teased.

Most times, he won because his legs, although skinny, were much longer and stronger than hers. Mat would occasionally let Bree win on purpose. He realized early on, the agony she dealt with at the house.

"What are you going to get Mat?" Bree asked as they walked to the double screen doors of the store.

"I am going to get some candy and cookies. You know the ones I get all the time."

"I don't know yet bighead, I've got to see first what they have, Bree, Bree," Matthew said and showed his victory smile that seemed to have extended for a mile.

Bree and Mat stocked up on their favorite penny candies from the plastic jars behind the displayed cases. Tootsie rolls, tootsie roll pops, Mary Janes, banana splits, squirrel nut zippers, and all the b-b-bats taffy pops (strawberry, banana, vanilla, and chocolate). Rows and rows of mouthwatering thinly sliced ginger snaps, as well as coconut and vanilla cookies. The coconut was Bree's favorite, and Matthew loved the ginger snaps. They decided to get ten of each and they would have them for later when they sat on the porch and played checkers. Bree got two pieces of the red-hot vinegary sausages, and Matthew got one of the pink pig's feet from the other jar on the counter by the cash register.

"Good afternoon, Mrs. Dunbar," Bree and Matthew said in unison.

"How are your folks doing, child?" Mrs. Dunbar

directed her question to Bree. She was not particularly fond of Matthew and his strong northern accent.

"They are doing good, Mrs. Dunbar," Bree projected an extra level of concern although thoughts of how her parents were doing were far away when she and her cousin rode to the store. Mr. Dunbar sat behind the potbelly stove that supplied warmth and comfort for the store and the attached house on cold winter days and nights in his favorite white rocking chair. He was not as friendly as Mrs. Dunbar. His attachment to southern white beliefs was always obvious in his facial expressions and reactions towards them.

When Bree and Matthew were in the store, and whites entered, he came to the counter and waited on them, and they knew to step aside and wait.

Matthew too often mumbled way too loud, "This is so stupid, why do we have to wait? We were here first."

Bree would nudge her cousin to let him know she heard his words, and so did mean old man Dunbar. It was an unwritten but an enforced rule of the Dunbar Country Store that colored customers had to wait until white customers were served. But their desires to have tasted the sweetness of the day was much greater than the racist rudeness of the nasty South they both agreed.

On the ride home, Bree tossed two pieces of the

sweetest, most sugary bubble gum in the South into her impatient mouth. Her mouth danced a jig with delight, as they rode their bikes slowly to have savored the taste of their delicious, delectable sweet treats. They rode their bikes in silence.

"Get up, go to that trash can, and spit that mess out," Mama commanded Bree. The loud pop reminded Mama she needed to have her weekly conversation about how she and the others were to have behaved in services for church on Sunday.

"Bree, Bree," Bree.

Bree knew when she said her name three times what followed next was a long drawn out and boring set of barked out orders on her behavior.

"Girl, gal, are you listening?"

"Yes, ma'am, I'm listening." Bree blew one more bubble before she emptied her mouth. Then she tried to have pulled it back in before it popped.

Pop. "Whoops," Bree said, but it was too late. The bubble popped, and the sound filled the entire kitchen once again. She felt Mama's body tighten with tension and knew without having to look. She had rolled her eyes.

"Lord, have mercy! Gal, you must have lost your mind just like your cousin. I'm so sick of you and that nasty stuff you keep chewing on and blowing those bubbles. Just rotting up your teeth."

"No ma'am," Bree said, answering a question that had not even been asked. This was Bree's go-to answer whenever Mama had a clothesline of questions. She cautiously uttered the response with a small smirk underneath her frowned face.

Mama's feet drug across the kitchen's floor as she moved toward Bree.

"Gal, sit up straight before I do the same thing to you and pop your tail."

A deep sigh with her hands on her hips.

"Tomorrow in church you better not think about chewing, smacking, blowing them bubbles, or eating any of that junk yawl got down there from that store, do you understand me? I see you from up there in the choir. You are going to sit on that second seat with Junior and Matthew and pay attention to every word Reverend Phillips preaches about, because Lord knows yawl need it. Yes, Lord," The old witch's voice sounded like someone was scratching on glass.

Bree responded with a nonchalant.

"Yes, ma'am." She drew out the ma'am, and this time rolled her eyes.

Reverend Phillips was an important relative of Bree's family. He was one of the most affluent ministers in the South, and he wore his affluence like a badge of pride and arrogance. Reverend Phillips also wore his ignorance and conceit just like his bodacious three-piece suits, wing-tipped matching shoes, and derbies that looked like top hats. He owned a long and big black Sedan Cadillac that he drove to four different churches where he preached his extended and lack-lustered sermons. He had built his business on preaching to one church for each Sunday of the month. He always found time to have visited the ranch for holiday meals and on the fifth Sundays of the month when he took a break from the selling of the Lord's word. He sat and communed with the family as if he had already made it to the pearly gates.

On his rare visits to the house he drew puffs of smoke that made him drunken from the smell that permeated from his gigantic hand-carved wooden smoking pipe. Smells that soaked up his sense of self. He sat on the long leather sofa by the window and cocked his head to one side as he took in deep draws from the pipe. The pipe hung from the side of his small slanted mouth. A small mouth that spoke so many big lies. Telling lies must have been his job because it certainly had buttered his bread on both sides.

Bree thought of how he bragged about on Sunday afternoons when he drove his old, long, customized black Cadillac and visited the sick and shut-in members and widows to spread his word while he collected their church dues. Daddy kept his cousin's pockets lined with green in a hope and a prayer that

23

someday it would be his green card through heaven's pearly gates. Both her parents thought the sun rose, and the moon sat whenever Reverend Phillips said it would. The family flauted Rev.'s prestige like it was their own.

Bree's confinement in front of the hot stove Saturday after Saturday for lengthy and painful hours affected her self-worth as she became older. The complete dismissiveness of the true natural way she had been born. Bree hated with a passion the moments she sat with her head bowed, and her self-respect diminished. But Mama relished the pleasures she found in the Saturday afternoon transformation of her uninhibited tomboyish daughter into a more feminine and softer being.

At an early age, Bree did not understand why her coils and natural curls had to be straightened and transformed into slicked back greasy pigtails. Her naturally thick and coarse tresses were a crown of springy coils that danced in the wind whenever she ran and played outside.

"Now that's better, look at you, go in there and wash that grease off your face."

In her mind, Bree thought sarcasticly, "How can I look at me, without a mirror?" For the last two hours, Bree had sat through the tormented ordeal and Mama's updates of the latest community gossip.

She rushed to the bathroom in the hallway, and washed the stains of sweat and grease from her face.

Bree threw the rag in the sink, and with her spirit lifted she skipped through the kitchen and out the back door.

"Free at last, Free at last, thank God all mighty, I'm free at last," Bree shouted as she danced out of the kitchen to the back porch. Matthew waited for her at the bottom step of the porch with a double-wide smile from ear to ear.

"Ready, set, go! Bree and Mat shouted and took off with full speed to the swing.

"I got here first, move Mat, stop it, Matthew, I mean it stop," Bree fussed with her cousin about who would have swung first in the makeshift swing that hung in the humongous Magnolia tree in the backyard. At her request Daddy created what Bree saw as a little haven for her to have read and be alone when Cousin Matthew was not visiting. A thick and worn rope was hoisted across the tree's strongest trunk, and an old tire once used to transport crops from the fields was tied to the lowest end.

"I hate your hair like that, trying to look like those white girls at the store," Matthew would say to his cousin when she had beaten him to the tire.

"Shut up, you always got something to say."

He teased his cousin when her hair was straightened because he liked it better when it was fluffy and looked like the clouds. Bree pushed Matthew, and he fell to the ground. She laughed out loud as she remembered when he had run into the backdoor of the house.

"What are you laughing at, with your old big-box head?" Matthew said while he lifted his body from the ground, and used the side of the tree for support.

"Ha, he, he, shut up. You get on my nerves. Remember when you hit the screened door, you forgot about the screen and ran head first into it?" Bree laughed, and so did Mat.

"Take your turn so I can get on, with your greasy head. Your head looks even bigger now, especially your fore head," Mat said playfully.

Bree continued to laugh at her cousin. Matthew had developed a heavy northern accent, although he had mostly grown up in the South with their Grandma Lilly. But his old southern charm magnetized and snapped Bree out of her anger toward him every time she had gotten upset. Bree smiled even when he teased and picked on her to the point of crying. Mat and Bree teased each other in fun but, he defended her when Junior started. Junior's teased bouts were nasty and heartless. Like the nastiness Mat saw in his uncle Wallace. Junior called Bree Blackie, and Ugly like it was her first and last names. His vulgar words irritated Matthew and made his skin crawled with fury.

"Touch me, touch me, Lord Jesus, touch me, Lord Jesus, with thy hand of mercy, guide me guide me,

Jehovah," Bree heard Mama as she sang and wiped the kitchen counters and the table. When she had reached for the broom in the corner, the words of the old Baptist hymn grew louder and clearer. This was one of the many hymns sung by the Senior Choir at New Ebenezer Missionary Baptist Church. The old hymnal was written ages ago by the Angelic Gospel Singers, and sung by so many choirs to mask pains and heartbreaks of the segregated South. Bree felt the song was a testimony of the pain Mama had endured being married to Daddy.

Oh, how Reverend Phillips did his greatest performances at funerals, anniversaries, or regular Sunday services when the Phillips Senior Choir struck up that song. He started by rocking in the seat, sat aside just for him. The red velveteen cushions matched the red carpet that covered the baptism pool. The louder the choir sang, the more he rocked and swayed from side to side until he could not have restrained the spirit of the demon that was in him. As he lunged to his feet, he commenced running from the pulpit to the pews. Lord, the energy from the deacons to the deaconess, to the ushers to both choirs boiled over, and the church became a heated mangled mess of entertainment for Bree, Junior, and Matthew during the week-long summer revivals. Mama's shadow appeared at the swing where Bree and Matthew sat and ate cookies and candies from their brown paper bags. The high pitch in Mama's voice made the hair on Bree's neck stand at attention.

"Get back on that porch, find a spot, and sit your little fast tail down. I have not done all that work on your head for nothing. Start running around out here in this heat, and sweat out them curls."

"Yes ma'am," Bree said and got up from the swing.

She and Matthew slowly followed Mama to the porch. Disappointed, they drug their feet across the porch, and found a chair at the far end. Matthew wanted to laugh but caught himself because he knew his aunt would not have spared him any mercy. Technically he was a guest at the ranch, but in his aunt's eyes, that had not mattered. The rod was not spared because of his temporary stay. He quickly sat in the rocking chair across from Bree, and they both stared in the direction of the tree and swing they had hoped to have swung on for the remainder of the day.

Bree's thoughts drifted off as she absorbed her mind into space. Why does she talk about people so much, why doesn't she ever talk to me, why doesn't she explain life to me instead of Mat telling me all these strange stories? Why is she so cotton-picking mean?

All the alone times they had together since Bree's birth, seldom if ever generated or planted seeds of worthwhile knowledge. Seeds that could have been sown and would have helped her to have a more balanced and stable perspective of life, and would have helped to developed a woman that understood her role and place in the world.

But for that moment, Bree knew she had better set

her little tail on the porch as she was told, or the skin that cried out from the closeness of the heat of the straightening comb could have turned and become the skin on her behind. Mama said what she meant and meant what she said. She handled her business about behavior, whether day or night, at the house or in the streets, or on the church pew, Bree Junior, and Matthew knew.

Today Matthew and Bree sat on the porch and switched between checkers and Old Maids. They ate some of the cookies they had bought and drank the grape sodas she had gotten from the refrigerator. Bree looked forward to beating her cousin at checkers, the game he loved so much.

"You cheated, you can't move there, you know that isn't how the game is supposed to be played," Matthew protested to his cousin every single time they played. Bree mocked his words and grinned her sneaky grin. I got you beat.

"Get over it, cousin, I won again," laughter. Bree danced her victory dance around Mat's rocking chair and hoped Mama had not looked out the window.

"Okay, you got me. That was a slick move, you little slicker.

"Dang, girl you cheat worse than me."

"I bet you think you are the best thing since sliced bread."

"I got you next time, you old trickster."

The checkers were reset on their appropriate side of the checkerboard, and the new game began. They played the afternoon away until finally, they heard;

"Time to eat. Yawl come on in here."

"Go wash your hands."

The old wicked witch of the South summoned everyone to the kitchen.

The kitchen table sat in the center of the bay windows and French doors that separated it from other areas of the house. Bree saw Matthew's nose when it perked up and pointed him to the table. She smiled because he looked like the Bassett Hound dog Grandpapa Sydney used when he hunted wild animals for the Sunday dinner table. The catfish was fried to a crispy and delicious brown delightfulness, and the smell still lingered heavy in the house. Stove topped cornbread gave a different smell as it was taken from the top of the stove and placed next to the pitcher of sweet lemonade garnished with fresh lemons. They sat and ate the delicious feast with minimal bouts of conversations. When words were spoken, the focus was on Daddy and his wheeling and dealings.

"You know, Berta, those cows are going to need to be taken to the market here soon. I have got to make room for those new calves that'll be here in the Spring," Daddy said with pride like he was the father.

"Yea, it's about that time of the year for some more." Mama chimed in to have shown some interest, and to have revived the conversation with some life support.

Bree and Matt looked at each other and hunched up their shoulders, but they quickly moved their eyes back to their plates to have finished the delicious meal. Junior could have cared less than less about any of this foolish family stuff. He finished his plate, leaned back in his chair, and waited for Daddy's gesture to have them all dismissed from the table.

"Yawl, go out and sit on the porch until it gets dark," these words were the cue they needed.

Junior ventured outside and sat in the swing at the opposite end of the porch from Bree and his not so favorite cousin. Bree and Matthew went for one more round of checkers. This time, Matthew was determined he would have won.

"Why yawl always playing that old stupid game?" Junior sat and taunted them. He would not have admitted it, but he felt left out.

"I'm going down to the pond and catch me a mess of fish," Junior announced to have gotten their attention.

"Go, nobody cares what you do, but if Mama finds out, she's going to beat your butt," Bree said like she had taken Mama's place.

31

"Oh, shut up, you talk too much, always trying to tell on somebody. Ya'll stay here and play that old dumb game for suckers," Junior said and hopped down off the side of the porch. He stayed in his own world disconnected from the family, absorbed in his own company.

The older Bree had gotten, the more she felt something just was not all there. Pieces of the puzzle were out of place. Time spent alone in her private little haven made her think more and more that she was not a part of her family's picture. Cousin Matthew's short visits provided more of a sense of connectedness to him and him only. A dysfunctional family picture that when the negatives were developed, she was captured in a frame of faked smiles.

Matthew and Bree's relationship grew closer and closer as years slowly but surely drifted away. When the summers ended and Matt was no longer there, Bree withdrew into the cocoon she had built as a protective barrier from the emotional agony of Mama, Daddy and her obnoxious brother. A retreat that was snugly tucked away, and used to have escaped her family's world.

One late afternoon, after Cousin Matthew had gone back, Bree rested peacefully in the comfort of her cocoon in the tire swing. She looked past the tree's canopied tops and its scented magnolia blossoms and saw a beauty only Mother Nature at her best could have created. Her mind pondered the notion of being re-incarnated somehow. That she had been here before, and in reality, this was not her family or her life. The more the thoughts invaded her mind, the greater her emotions grew. She searched her soul for the answer as if looking for gold. Tears welled and swelled in her big brown and not so vibrant eyes. Bree turned towards the sky's shielded sun light, and bellowed a demand for the universe to have spoken.

"Who am I? Who am I? Who am I? " Bree demanded three times as if three times was the magical charm that was needed for her requested answer. She believed with all that was in her heart, that something just wasn't right.

These strong and powerful feelings of what felt like "déjà vu" doused the serenity of the day. Fires of thoughts and emotions raged, and the flames were fanned with bitterness.

The cocoon that protected her for the first twelve years of her life developed within her a strong resilience. Her protection within it's walls taught her which battles needed to be fought, how to have gone with the flow of the waves and not to have fought the tides, when to have been brave, and when to just have enjoyed the ride.

Bree often sat in her most favorite place in the world and read by herself after Matthew had gone back. She quenched her thirst with escapes through magazines she had gotten from the mailbox. Her family brought no savory substance to the table that would have helped seasoned her hungry mind. Mama only knew community gossip and the Bible. Bree's thoughts jumped to an unpleasant moment of gossip her Mama had repeated.

"Child, you know some of these folks around here are going to go to hell in a handbasket if they don't straighten up and fly right. Around here, sneaking and creeping, slipping and hiding, gliding and diving like they don't have any sense. Because heaven is the place, I know and want to go." Words Mama spoke like she knew she was on her way to heaven.

Bree thought, *not unless the rules change, you aren't going nowhere near heaven, with your mean self.* All she knew and talked about was dying, heaven, hell, and what was wrong with everyone other than herself and that man she called her husband.

"Mama why do you talk so much about dying, what about life and living right now? Sounds so weird," Bree questioned Mama one day with boldness while she straightened her hair.

"You just don't know, child, you don't understand the ways of this old world, and the cries of the walls of this house," Mama said and reached for the dish rag that rested by the sink.

"No, I don't," Bree mumbled.

Only ideas of how she felt she was not a part of where she existed.

TROUBLED WATERS

Bree skipped across the front yard and suddenly stopped. She heard Daddy when he shouted in her direction.

"Come here, gal! Get your tail over here right now! Right now! Lord have mercy, Jesus. You are going to be the death of me. Fannie Mae called here and said she had to whip your tail because you were over there cussing and carrying on like you was grown and don't have any home training or sense. She said you and those children of hers took some of old man Sammy's chewing tobacco. What did you do with that tobacco?"

Bree dropped her head down to the ground in order to have not made eye contact with Daddy.

"It's gone, Mrs. Fannie Mae took the rest from Sammy," Bree nervously said to Daddy.

Bree and her friends, Sammy Jr., and Rachel wondered what the tobacco tasted like since Mr. Sammy always had some stuffed inside his mouth that poked out his jaws and made them rounded. It seemed as if anytime he was walking, talking, or laughing. He was chewing. He sat on the porch with a mouth full and chewed the dark brown plugs of loose-leaf tobacco that smelled so sweet, and spat the juice clear across the porch in what seemed to be a mile in front of him. These gestures intrigued Bree, Sammy, and Rachel.

"Sammy, you do it, you go get it, the chewing tobacco, it's on the table, nobody is going to see you," Bree convinced Sammy to have done the dirty deed.

Bree and Rachel waited outside on the back porch by the old wringer wash machine that had not been used in years. When the Johnson's bought a new machine, they abandoned the old one and placed it on the back porch of the house. Sammy completed the task and trotted back out the house. He pulled the treat from the front pocket of his pants. All three looked at each other and laughed with anticipation of what was ahead. They made a mad dash to the opened field beyond the nicely manicured yard Mr. Johnson took the greatest of pride in. Each of them in their own little unique minds raced to have found out what Mr. Sammy loved so much about the gushy glob that pushed his jaws to have looked like inflated balloons. The excitement grew when Sammy pulled the package's sealed top and grabbed a hand full of the delightful smell. He handed Bree and his sister a handful for them to have tasted.

Sammy was the first to have spoken, "Not bad, right?"

Bree and Rachel both nodded in agreement.

"Give me some more," Bree stuck out both hands like the contents Sammy handed her was heavy.

"Wait, Bree, give me a minute, dang, wait," Sammy said over and over, and Rachel waited with patience.

Little had they known that Mrs. Fannie Mae saw Sammy, and trailed them to the end of the yard. She watched in the distance without ever having said a word.

"Damn, this stuff is good, damn good," Bree said after she had partially aimed and spat the first juices on the ground. The brown juice that had missed the ground landed on front of her white blouse.

"Oh, hell, damn," Bree continued as the others laughed. The adventure of the moment continued until her stomach started to hurt.

"I feel bad.""What's wrong with you?" Rachel asked. Bree had seen Mr. Sammy chewed and spat the juices from the tobacco for years, but she soon realized from the rumbles in her stomach she had swallowed more than she had spat.

"That stuff is good as--" Sammy started but never finished.

Mrs. Fannie Mae's face said it all. The three knew the pains that bubbled in their stomachs had just turned to a different kind of pain. But for Bree, the journey to pain had just begun. She had more pain to be gained when she reached the house.

Bree stood in front of Daddy without having to look him directly in his face. She knew from the experiences of the past, what the fate was once the questions were done.

"What do you have to say for yourself, gal?"

Well, old man, if you know the answers, why do you keep asking me the same dumb questions? Bree thought to herself. But she played the role of acting dumbfounded to his questions for as long as possible, avoiding the inevitable.

"Sir, I mean yes, sir. I did."

"Did what gal?"

"Um, I was cussing and saying things I should not have been saying and chewing tobacco with Sammy and them."

Daddy took several steps toward Bree and planted his feet firmly into the dirt that stood between them. Bree kept her head down as she tried and failed to take a step back. She felt the rumbles and churns in the pit of her stomach. Her mouth became filled with thick saliva as sweat covered her dirty face.

"Lord knows I get more and more disappointed in you every day you walk on this earth. If only you had been born."

The pains and sickness Bree felt in her stomach started to move upward as the sweat now covered her entire body.

"I prayed and prayed for you to had been born-"

Bree's eyes crept up and met Daddy's before he had finished his words. Before she knew it she had vomited on his shoes.

"Get in that house," his sharp and deep voice boomed. "Fannie Mae, better not ever call this house again about you and your foolishness; you hear me, gal?" Her Father looked at his shoes disgusted.

Sniffing and pushing back tears, Bree mumbled, "Yes, sir."

After an hour of sulking in her room and nursing her stomach back to life from the tobacco and two spankings, Bree moved slowly pass Mama while she silently looked out of the kitchen's window, her back to Bree. The green plant that surrounded the window's sill and created a halo of greenery around Mama was not as appealing today. Bree stood behind her Mama's back with waves of anger because she had not protected her. Then Mama blurted out more pain.

"Where in the world did you get that filthy mouth from, girl?"

Underneath her breath, Bree muffled, "You, where do you think?" She rolled her eyes in the direction of the window.

"Go out there and sit on that porch until I tell you to get up."

"Yes ma'am," Bree said, and the door slammed behind her.

Bree pushed herself back and forth in the swing at the end of the long porch. She felt she needed to be as far away from them as possible. "What did he mean, when he said he wishes I had been born and did not finish? Born what, or did he mean never born?" The emotional pain at this point was so much greater than her physical pain. From the outer edge of the porch. Bree heard an angry voice from the raised window in the kitchen.

"Berta, I wish that child had never been born, you know. You know how much I wanted another boy. She is as black as the shoes on my feet with all that nappy hair on her head. Hair looking like those wiry pads you use to scrub pots and pans with. I just wanted a son. Then she came here. Why don't she have skin bright and hair like them other gals? Lord knows she will never find anybody that want to marry her."

Daddy moved away from the window but continued his conversation with Mama. Bree got up and sneaked to the opened window. She pressed her back against the house, and turned her head in the direction of the uncomfortable conversations.

"Berta, you know that child is going to be the death of me. Every since she got here; it's just been one thing after another."

"Well, it's your fault Wallace. If you hadn't. Lord have mercy Jesus. Don't blame this on that child. She didn't ask to come here."

"Hadn't what woman? You always bringing up the past. Always digging your nose up in my business."

Bree overheard her parents as they argued about her. She slid down the side of the wall and sat on the floor of the porch.

This was not the first time she had unintentionally overheard exchanges between them and Mama's sister about her. Secret conversations about her and her suspicious birth.

Bree thought just as the old folks said, "Something in the milk wasn't clean."

Bree's birth was a sticky topic, especially when Daddy so blatantly expressed his needs to have had his precious second son.

BIRTH OR NOT

"Roberta, I have a great concern about your health, and you trying to have another baby. I think you and Wallace should consider not trying again. This is not good on your body," Dr. Young cautioned, Roberta in his office during her check-up after her fourth miscarriage. "Your body needs time to heal."

She shuddered to think what her husband's reaction would be when he heard the news from the doctor. As the air condition blasted in the front seat of the Cadillac, Berta rehearsed how she would share the bad news.

She finally said, "We can't try no more."

Wallace spoke his peace. "He doesn't know what he's talking about. We are going to keep trying woman. Your body is still young and strong."

Like it was his body and his womb, that big fat primitive mind told him he needed his heirloom son.

Three months later Wallace drove Roberta to Dr. Young's office again. She had complained of being tired, nauseous, and crankier than usual.

"Well, Roberta, look like you didn't listen to my warning. You are pregnant again. But you are going to have to be really careful and take it easy this time. Believe and know this is going to be a rough ride because of the four miscarriages already."

The half-day wait in the colored only section of the doctor's office had been a tiring enough ordeal for Roberta by itself. All the white patients were called to the back before black patients were thought of, even if they arrived and signed in before white patients. After she had gathered her composure and her oversized pocketbook, Roberta took the long and dark walk back to the sign-in desk where the attending and only black nurse dropped her off to have paid her bill. The plump and semi-friendly receptionist behind the plastic glass window greeted her with a semi-friendly smile.

"That'll be fifty dollars, Roberta. Now we will need to see you back in two weeks. You are a high-risk case; you know?"

"Yes, ma'am, two weeks," she responded to the receptionist with disappointment in her voice.

The sun beamed high in the sky, but dark clouds loomed around Roberta as she took what seemed to have been the walk of an eternity. Wallace sat impatiently on the driver's side of the car as she opened the passenger side door.

Sighs rushed into the car's silence.

"What did they say?"

"Well, I'm expecting again but," before she had finished her words, Wallace interrupted.

"Good, another boy, I bet." Wallace's face lit up the

sky on the hot summer's afternoon even brighter.

Roberta turned her body and attention to the passenger window. The beautiful landscapes she viewed on the ride to the doctor's office changed to, blurred visions, impaired by tears that had swelled in her eyes. She thought of the physical pain of the miscarriages, one after the other. The loneliness and sadness she felt after each loss of life.

That night after supper, Roberta decided to have finished the conversation she had started in the car.

"Dr. Young said this child won't be easy to carry because of all the other losses."

For the first time since the visit, he showed signs of being concerned. Not so much concerned for Roberta, but for having another loss.

"You are not going to go back to that old crazy doctor, "Wallace told Roberta sternly. She realized she had no say so whatsoever.

She knew not to have said anything, and just went about clearing and cleaning the kitchen. At the end of her cleaning, she walked slowly to the bedroom, and sat in silence in the dark. Roberta's body language smelled of thick distress.

Seven and a half months after that despairing night, Berta's body was wrapped and covered in horrific pain. She felt as if she had been twisted, pulled, and squeezed out of a tube.

"Help me! Help me Lord Jesus!" The baby was on the way early.

Wallace heard Bertha's screams and ran to call the only mid-wife in the small community, Mrs. Lucille.

"Hello, is this you Lucille? "He was hysterical as screams covered the bedroom.

"Yes, sir.

"It's Berta!"

"I'm on my way."

Mrs. Lucille arrived at the house, and jumped out of the car before the car had been placed in park. Her body moved faster than her feet was able to have kept up with. The battered black bag that was used so many times to have brought so many other babies into the world was grabbed from the back seat of the car.

"E-e-e-e-ouch, Lord have mercy, Jesus," Roberta screamed and moaned. During the months she had carried the child, she had not returned to Dr. Young's office for any of her scheduled followed-up examinations. She left the house less and less, and made her appearance very minimal, even at church.

Mrs. Lucille arrived within minutes after she was called. She waddled like a duck until she reached the bedroom's entrance, and was out of breath as she turned the knob without knocking.

"She's in there Lucille."

Mrs. Lucille pushed past Wallace and entered the room panting hard and out of breath.

"Mrs. Berta, Mrs. Berta I'm here. I'm here and everything is going to be all right."

Mrs. Lucille moved to the foot of the bed, and started her work.

"Push, push. Push harder Berta," Mrs. Lucille the older heavy-set mid-wife repeatedly shouted with a heavy southern drawl from the foot of the queen-sized bed.

Berta's spirit had not matched the Queen title that was given to the bed she laid helplessly in. She felt nothing like a Queen when a final push was mustered up. The scream sounded unlike any Mrs. Lucille had ever heard.

"Oh, my holy Jesus," Mrs. Lucille's face went blank with an unsettled and disturbed look. The new addition to the family was here, but something was wrong.

After he had waited as patiently as he knew how Wallace knocked on the closed door. When Mrs. Lucille opened the bedroom door, he practically fell to the floor but grabbed the wall. Then, without waiting for an answer, he walked into a situation he

47

was not at all ready to have experienced.

"What's going on?

What happened?" He questioned Mrs. Lucille, and was mortified when she said.

"It's a girl," Mrs. Lucille announced to the room. But something else was not quite right.

"I need some more time, Mr. Breeze. I need you to leave, leave now!" Mrs. Lucille repeated with force and demand. Roberta felt the air thicken with discontent that now permeated through her husband's eyes, and body language as he slowly left the room.

He had bragged and boasted every chance and opportunity he had gotten uncontrollably for the past months about "his new baby boy. Junior was not talked about because he had been placed on the replacement list. The physical pain from the birth was hardly any match for the obvious egotistical setback he displayed as he left the room.

"I'm finished Mrs. Berta, just need to clean up these towels and put them in the laundry bag," Do you want me to get Mr. Breeze? Mrs. Lucille decided she would say as less as possible.

She worked in silence after her one and only question.

"Yes, I guess so." Roberta said with great reluctance.

He returned to the room, but did not speak. Just looked spell bounded as he glared at the new addition to the family. Roberta's eyes looked beyond where he stood at the foot of the bed, and into the mirror that sat on the dresser. She caught a glimpse and saw a sad and broken face that looked back.

FOR BETTER OR WORSE

After they were married at an early age in the spring of 1955, Mama and Daddy moved into a very small four-room house in the middle of miles and miles of open land. In the fall of 1956, Junior was born to the delight of Daddy on a fall like afternoon. Mama's pains were powerful but short as Junior was ready to have made his entrance into the world. Daddy stood proudly over his wife because his pride and joy was finally here.

"Look at my boy, look just like me. He is going to help me with all this land and crops. Yeah, that boy is going to be running this place." He rambled on with all his hopes and dreams that would be carried out by Wallace Junior.

In the middle of his conversation with himself, Dr. Young interrupted and said, "Roberta needs her rest. She has been through a lot. You can come back tomorrow."

The trophy son that Wallace had bragged about so much, was born and destined to have carried on the Breeze legacy, to have run to the finished line with a lit torch. A perfectly innocent soul, brought into a harsh and unfair world already loaded down with burdens placed upon him because of the family he was born into. Junior never stood a chance in Daddy's world.

A simplistic life was created in the little house that

sat in the middle of open land separated from the rest of the town. The land was purchased by Daddy from old man Solomon Banks. Mr. Banks had fallen on hard times and needed the money. Therefore, Daddy got the property he wanted at a real steal, and eventually built a house that only a few in the town had one like.

Although in a segregated South with only a sixth-grade education, he was determined to make his marriage work and provide the best world for his family. He was also determined not to have worked for others, especially the affluent whites.

Mama's education ended early in her childhood, but she and Bree graduated from high school on the same humid night. Some things are taught and some things are learned. Both of Bree's parents as youths were pulled from school to have worked in the fields where they labored from sun up to sundown.

Mama was robbed of an opportunity to have been a loving wife and mother because of the man she had married. She held on to the bitter and raw pent up pains from the past letdowns of her childhood and a marriage that was more for worse than for better. The youthful peace she felt at the beginning of the marriage was replaced with discontentment as she found herself struggling in a daily storm. A life of hard knocks taught her to have tuned out the sounds of the house and her Daddy. Imaginary blinders shielded and protected her from the unpleasant views in the house. Blinders like the real ones worn by mules in the South that toiled the land, and plowed straight rows.

The young Wallace started and built his own business from the ground up. With the same strong-will and tenacity of the bulls that were bred and fed on his ranch. He gained his status in the community and became the first African American rancher and farmer in Allendale, SC. The types of crops Wallace grew on the one hundred acres of land not occupied by livestock, and their home was divided between front crops and back crops. He grew and harvested all sorts of crops. Front crops shielded the presence of the illegal crops that grew in the grassy green pastures beyond the cattle.

Early lessons taught Wallace how to have saved the money he needed to pay cash for over two hundred acres of uncharted land. The purchase of this amount of land during such a harsh time of white supremacy and black suppression fed Wallace's inflated ego as a black man in the South. He felt that he was not like other blacks in the small town.

Young and high on life, he ate up his opportunity of semi-acceptance into the white world like an appetizing plate of day-old collard greens with white rice and a good size, side of stove topped grilled cornbread. His new lifestyle turned him into more and more of a monster because of his greed and need. But he kept his money tight and right.

One sunny afternoon, six months after they had settled into their new home, a beautiful red convertible Corvette drove up the driveway and stopped just beyond the last Pecan tree.

"Who's that out there in the yard?" Mama screamed at Bree as she kicked her feet, and moved slowly on the wooden swing held with bolted chains.

"I don't know," Bree replied with a questionable tone and a hard look at the woman in the car. Bree's steps were slow when she moved toward the back door. She saw Mama from the porch with her face practically glued to the kitchen window

"Bree, is your Daddy out there?" Mama asked while she refocused on where Bree was.

"Come on in this house! Don't slam that door." Mama said as she stepped back from the window over the sink, and walked over to the stove.

She knew too well that when Mama used that tone, it had more to do with Daddy and not her. She entered the house and closed the door slowly behind herself. She took one last look at the beautiful light-skinned woman that sat in the fancy car.

"Here, child take a piece of this syrup bread while it's still hot."

Mama mumbled, "Bet that's that old floozy he's running around here with. Lord have mercy on both their old no good for nothing souls."

"That lady sure is pretty. Ain't she Mama? That's a nice car she's driving too." Bree said in order to have irritated Mama.

Mama heard Daddy's pick-up truck when he drove into the driveway.

"Shut that big fat fresh mouth of yours, before I whip that little grown tail," Mama said, this time with forceful anger. Bree smirked with delight as she quenched her appetite.

COUNTRY CRAZINESS: BOUGIE BLACKNESS

The Breeze Bunch became known around the town of Allendale as the bougie blacks. This feeling of superiority gave Daddy dearest, a pride that his status was different than other blacks in the small town. A certain level of equality to whites. The reality of it all was they were just merely true backwoods black, Beverly Hillbillies.

Bree watched through the door's screen as Mama and Daddy piled into the front seat of the blue Chevrolet pick-up truck. He had bought the pick-up two weeks earlier and paid cash. The smell of its newness clung to their clothes whenever they ran their errands or drove the many acres of the ranch's land. Mama sat as close to the door as possible in an effort to not have been near Daddy. He sat high and straight on his side with overzealous pride.

They were off to take the hour or so drive to Aiken, South Carolina for supplies. They needed items to be prepared for the winter when the new livestock arrived. The items he needed were not sold at Mr. Woods' Feed and Seed Store in the heart of the little town of Allendale. At least four times a year, the trip was made, and Bree and Junior were left alone with Junior as the keeper of the castle. Bree was not a fan of these times when Junior was supposed to be the babysitter. He tortured and taunted his sister with the foulest words he could have thought up about his sister's looks.

"You are so ugly you look like homemade sin. Always out there looking like a monkey sitting in a tree. You want a banana? You are so ugly you would make an onion cry."

It was if they were not brother and sister. These times were a reminder to Bree of all the whispers and secret conversations she had overheard about herself between her parents and aunt when she had come to visit Mama.

The new pick-up truck slowly vanished beyond the last Pecan tree at the end of the horseshoe shaped driveway. Junior ran into the kitchen and was out of breath, dirty, and wet from washing the piece of junk he called a car. He and Uncle Henry had rebuilt a replicated model of a 1965 Mustang from parts and a frame Uncle Henry had in his junkyard. Junior spent most of his time with his uncle and not Daddy, because Uncle Henry was the cool uncle. Junior worshipped the ground he walked on because he smoked cigarettes, and blew smoke rings in the air.

"Man that's cool, Uncle Henry. Can I try?" Junior tried but never got his smoke to make a ring.

He drank gin from the bottle no matter what the hour of the day; cussed out anyone that crossed the line, and talked smack to everybody. Even white people when they pushed his buttons. But what Junior loved the most was when he told Daddy where to go, and it wasn't to heaven. They talked for hours about Daddy. Uncle Henry and Daddy both owned their own businesses, but Uncle Henry's business was not seen as prestigious as Daddy's because of the crowd that hung out in the junkyard.

Bree sat at the round table in one of the six high back chairs. A plate of chocolate chip cookies sat on the yellow floral placemat in front of her. She opened the refrigerator door and grabbed a chilled grape soda off the second rack. Junior showed absolutely no acknowledgments of his sister's presence, pushed past her and rushed for the spiral staircase

"Where are you going, stupid?"

"With your stink self."

"You know you are supposed to watch me while they are gone," she said rudely to her obnoxious brother.

"Yeah, whatever with your nappy head."

"They don't tell me what to do, and neither do you, you little tattletale," Junior barked back at his little sister.

She took the remainder of her snack and went into the sunlit den-like Mama had directed her. After a brief retreat to his room, Junior descended the stairs after changing into new clothes without bathing.

"You haven't wash with your stink self, "she laughed and teased her brother from the den. The floor model TV blasted Gilligan's Island in the background as Gilligan had made yet another bad decision and sabotaged their chances of being rescued.

Junior never really listened to his parents when they told him to have stayed and watched his sister. Bree ran from the room and shouted in Junior's direction.

"I'm telling if you leave," Bree screamed while she followed her brother to the door.

"Go ahead, you little rat I don't care if you do, all yawl can take a flying leap off a high cliff." Junior had heard his uncle used these words when he had gotten angry in the junkyard with people. He thought this was his time to have acted like his favorite uncle. He lunged off the back porch and ran to his friend, Keith's car. Keith was Junior's white friend. Junior slammed the passenger side door of the car, and Keith mashed the gas pedal to the floor. Dirt with gravel rocks from the driveway's edge casted a dusted cloud at the back of the house.

Bree stood and watched as her brother and his friend drove away. She returned to the den where her plate and soda were completely empty. She took the plate and the can to the kitchen, and stood for a few moments trying to suppress the anger and refocuse her energy. The last ten minutes of Gilligan's Island, was only seen with a glance as she gazed beyond the TV's black and white screen and wished her favorite cousin was there. Wished they were outside fighting over who would have the first turn on the tire swing. She so needed his silliness and laughter.

The days, the months, the years became more and

more difficult for Bree. Daddy reminded her with harsh words about her looks. Words that were harder to have swallowed than the tart blackberries she and her cousin Matthew picked on the railroad tracks that looped at the back of the house.

Bree was headed to her seat at the kitchen table when Daddy's words were slung at her across the table.

"Look at you with all that nappy hair on your head, gal? Lord knows your Mama needs to comb your head with that hot comb. Looking like I don't know what. God knows you look rougher than a corn cob." Her spirit dropped to zero. Daddy spoke these words too often and too freely.

"You will always be stuck right here, no further than you are, looking like a boy with all those old boy clothes on and that bird nest head. Lord knows not a single soul is going to ever want you."

She kept her head down as Daddy continued his tirade of insults. Junior sat on the other side of the table and laughed out loud as he reared back in his chair. Mama stood at the sink with her back to them. Bree had hoped for once in her life Mama would have rescued her from this crazy man. Instead, she just washed the already clean dishes again.

After supper she went outside and finished the last chapter of her book while she swung back and forth in the old tire swing. She found a peaceful haven beneath the trees. She indulged herself with stacks

61

and stacks of reading, heaps of drawings she drew of impeccable landscapes, animals, and creatures she saw on the ranch.

Her greatest desire from deep down inside was to have been the pride and joy of her Mama and Daddy's eyes.

The house grew colder and lonelier for her as she grew more and more accustomed to the punishing harshness of her parents and brother. But this unpleasantness extended way beyond the walls of the Breeze household, and traveled with Bree when she entered other family's houses, when she was at school, and even in the place, she least expected, at church.

GRANNY CRAB APPLE

It was 4:00 p.m. Sunday afternoon, and every member of the Breeze family knew what this meant. The house was filled with rules, rituals, and routines that never wavered. It was time for the family to have piled into the big long Cadillac and visit her least favorite grandma, Grandma Mary. Bree called her Crabby Apple Granny because she was round, bitter, and always sour when it came to her. She had a cruel soul, and was as cold as the ice used to have chilled the sweet tea and lemonade, she and her cousin Mat drank on sultry hot summer days on the back porch when they took breaks from the heat of the day

"Grandma Mary is so mean; do I have to go? And do I have to wear this ugly dumb dress she made?" Bree protested.

Getting her to wear a dress for any occasion was a struggle, it was like a dentist pulling teeth without a pain killer.

"Please, can I please take this off?" Bree begged and pleaded as she stood in front of the floor-length mirror in the foyer. A slight moment of kind-heartedness came to Mama's eyes. The dress really was quite unattractive. But Mama said nothing as usual. She just gave in to the desires of Grandma Mary, although she was not a favorite of hers. Grandma Crabby Apple thought her precious and perfect son could have and should have done so

63

much better.

"You are going, and you are going to keep that dress on she made for you and you will tell your grandma, thank-you, ma'am. Put your shoes on so we can go and get back here before dark," Mama said and headed to the door.

Bree hated shoes. She loved the feel of the earth and her connection to it when she ran barefoot in the yard. "Where is Junior at? Junior, get down here!" Mama's shouts trailed up the stairs. Bree already knew where Junior was but kept silent. She had hoped his absence would have prolonged leaving the house so that less time was spent at her grandparents. Junior had left the house shortly after church without telling Mama or Daddy, and gone with his friends.

Mama looked in her direction and ask, "Where is Junior, child?"

Before she responded, Daddy crudely said as he looked at his spotless car.

"Ya'll get in the car. We have got to go. Don't worry about him. He can stay here with his hard head self. Head just as hard as that highway out there. But he's going to see how that hard head is going to make for a soft tail one of these days."

Daddy moved from that old grinning and skinning fool that sat in the deacon's section of New Ebenezer Missionary Baptist Church less than two hours ago to his normal beast mode.

The family gathered themselves in the car and found their assigned seats. Just as Bree was about to have closed her door, Junior grabbed the handle and pulled the door open. She nearly toppled to the ground.

"Move over out of my spot, girl, you know that's where I sit. Get out the way," Junior shouted and laughed at his sister as she clung to the door.

Daddy was furious. "Where have you been, boy? You always find a way to get on that one last nerve I got left."

"I was down by the pond. Why? Old man, are you mad?" Junior snapped at Daddy.

"Just get in and shut the door. We are already late, thanks to you."

Junior sighed and smiled at the back of the head that held the big round hat. He slammed the door as hard as he possibly could have.

"You look like a piece of burnt toast that somebody threw up?" Junior teased Bree from the back seat for the entire thirty minutes of the ride. "That's the ugliest dress I have ever seen; look like that pink stuff you take when your stomach is hurting. What do you have on, that thing is uglier than you. Neither of her parents said a word to Junior in fear he would have lashed out on them.

The pink laced dress Grandma Mary had made, was

for her to have worn on the 25th Church Anniversary of New Ebenezer Missionary Baptist Church. Grandma Mary spent hours on the old-fashioned foot pedaled sewing machine she had used to have sown her own clothes, and made Bree's dress so that Sister Laura could have seen her work.

Might as well have called the church, The Breeze Missionary Baptist Church the way they carried on and flaunted around in it. Every pew that one of the Breeze family members sat on seemed to have carried some kind of royalty and prestige in the church, at least so they thought. They sat with their backs straight with an air of pride, heads held high, and noses turned up at those that sat near. Junior sat slouched in his seat as an act of defiance. He stared at his parents and never made eye contact with old good for nothing Reverend Phillips. Bree watched from the side and observed her parent's reaction to Junior. She laughed inside.

Wallace drove into his favorite spot under the Magnolia tree. He felt the shade of the tree's branches would have protected it from the heat of the day. Bree looked so forward to seeing her Grandpa Sydney on these Sunday visits, but not so much Grandma Mary. They waited on the front porch for the family's arrival. Bree smiled when she saw Grandpa Sydney sitting in the rocking chair. After the car was parked, Daddy piloted the crew to the porch.

Grandma Mary stood a plump and round five feet

five tall. She balanced the extra weight she carried on all parts of her body very attractively. Her oval face was covered with dark age splotches from the southern summer's heat. On Sundays she would cover the splotches with make-up that never matched her skin.

"How yawl doing?" Grandpa Sydney's words were warm and his smile inviting.

Grandpa Sydney was the wisest one of the family, and somehow managed to always have a joke ready at the drop of a dime. He stood an inch taller than Grandma Mary, but for Bree, he seemed so much bigger. He had not changed out of his tailored suit pants, shirt, tie, and vest Grandma Mary had made him for the church's anniversary. His smile beyond his full lips and the cigar he clenched between his teeth showed the straight rows of teeth stained from all the years of smoking cigars and pipes.

Grandma Mary had gone back to the kitchen to have checked on Sunday's dinner.

She opened the front door just as Grandpa Sydney's hand grabbed the knob of the screen door. The house was flawlessly kept. Everything had a place and was always in its place.

"How yawl doing?"

"Come on in, come on in."

"Lord, it's hot. Ya'll doing all right?"

"Sit-down." Grandma Mary said to the family as she ushered them into the living room. The family took their familiar seats.

"We are good, Mama. Pappa how are you doing, sitting out there in all that heat?" Daddy greeted Grandma and Grandpa.

"That sure was a good sermon Reverend Phillips preached, wasn't it?" Grandma Mary said with proudness.

"Yeah, it was. He knows his way around that Bible. Sure enough preached a good sermon today. Yes, indeed," Daddy responded.

If anyone had asked him what it was about, he would not have had the first clue. He never could move beyond those words, "He, sure enough can, preach that Bible."

Bree laughed as she thought about all the Sundays they rode back from church, and he tested Junior and her about the sermon.

"Girl, what did the preacher preach about today?" They would look at each other, and would quietly say with a laugh, "You don't know, we could say anything." One of few times, Junior and Bree shared a laugh about their coo-coo old Daddy.

The smells of Grandma Mary's Sunday afternoon

feast slapped Bree in the face. Her mouth watered, and her stomach rumbled like the thunder that was often heard in the far distance on late summer evenings. The smells summoned them to the dining room table. Bree moved quickly to her favorite chair in hopes that Junior would not have been any place near her. The chair faced the window, and from her seat, she saw the apple orchards and pear trees, the open fields beyond the trees, and Grandpa Sydney's Basset Hounds. The new puppies basked in the Sunday afternoon sun as they were fed by their mother. Grandpa Sydney filled his time from the house and away from Grandma Mary with hunting and fishing. He brought home rabbits, raccoons, birds, deer, and messes of fresh fish.

Bree's picture of what a marriage should be was unclear based on what she saw from her parents and grandparents. Her grandparent's actions toward each other were even stranger, a strange weirdness that stood out like a Christmas tree being lit on the Fourth of July in the South. A marriage that had survived over a half-century of wars and the Great Depression, the emergence of their ten descendants, and descendants of their own. But Bree never felt or saw love and affection between them.

"Gal, I need you to come here, I got something for you to do," Grandma Mary shouted from the far corner of the kitchen.

Bree entered the kitchen where Grandma Mary stood

in front of the massive stove. On the stove she saw four pots that seemed synchronized to the same beat. The tall pot although deeply stained and dented from constant cooking, boiled fresh butter beans with freshly-cut okras. The pot's twin, sat on the opposite side and simmered with fresh turnip greens and the sweet smell of the pinch of sugar she had added. The hot grease in the old cast iron frying pan splattered and spilled over as Grandma Mary removed the crispy golden-brown fried chicken to the serving platter.

"Go put this on the table child, and come back and get these other plates," Grandma Mary barked at Bree.

"Yes, ma'am. I'll be right back." Bree was ready to eat the delights she carried so faithfully to the table. She pinched a piece of the crispy treat, and quickly pushed it into her mouth.

"Mmm, that's good." Bree speedily moved back to the kitchen.

Old Crabby Granny Apple had made three stacks of golden-brown stove top cornbread with complete perfection. Each piece of the stack had been flipped and turned without a torn or broken corner.

"Put this cornbread on the table by the greens."

"Yes, Grandma."

Bree did as she was directed and placed each dish in

its place. Grandma Mary followed her with hot platters of macaroni and cheese and baked chicken. She returned to the kitchen and placed the baked raccoon with sweet potatoes on a platter. This was her favorite son's favorite dish.

"Child, go in there and get that tater salad and white rice." Grandma Mary's Sunday meal was not a completed treat without these two items.

The six scrumptious sweet potato and coconut pies, cooked from Grandma Mary's secret recipe, sat on the counter and cooled. They would be eaten after dinner with a scoop of her homemade lemon ice cream.

The entire time Bree was in the kitchen with Grandma Mary, she never said a word about the dress she had made. Although she had despised the idea of wearing a dress, especially this pink looking tablecloth, she thought something would have been said about her prized work.

Uncle Henry's family still had not arrived, and dinner had been placed on the table. While they waited impatiently, Grandma Mary walked back to the kitchen under the pretense that she needed something she had missed putting on the table.

"Come here, child, I got something for you from the store yesterday." Grandma Mary said flusterd that Uncle Henry was late again.

Bree stood over the pies on the table with the plastic tablecloth, and twiddled her thumbs around each other. She had the look and feel she had every Christmas when it was time to have opened gifts. From the cream-colored apron's pocket, her grandma had worn since their arrival, she pulled out a neat little brown box.

"Child, I got something for you to use on your face that is going to make your skin look lighter."

"Lighter? What does that mean?" Bree was confused.

Her eyes searched frantically for Mama in the dining room. Where was she when she needed her to have explained this or at least have saved her from this awkward moment? She caught a glimpse of Mama in the dining room. She sat on the opposite end of the dining room table, as far away as she could have possibly been from Daddy, and pretended to have listened to the exchanges about the weather and when the heat would have changed.

"Child, your skin is as dark as night. It don't look good like that. Skin is ugly when it's dark like yours. Take this box. I use this on my skin. Use this, and your skin will be the color of your Mama's." Grandma Mary, tried to have explained.

What is this crazy old woman talking about? Confused.

"What's wrong with my skin?"

Bree's dark, smooth and silky skin was too often mocked, and was the repugnant joke at the family's Sunday dinners.

For a brief moment in the kitchen, thoughts of how this was a turning point for her and Grandma Mary, excited Bree. But the weird chat proved to have been the complete opposite, and ruined what would have been a semi-good day with Grandpa Sydney. Bree was mortified, and what was left of her high spirit hit a low spot. While some things often changed in life, life with Grandma Mary remained the same.

Bree's mind reminisced about one of the rare occasions' when the family sat for their evening supper and Daddy shared and spoke openly about Granny Crabby. On this particular Sunday, she had belittled him in front of everyone at the table, and he was furious.

"Sitting over there thinking you the man, boy you better remember where you came from," Grandma Crabby said in the rudest way she knew while she stared Daddy in the face. He sucked up the words with the greatest of pain and embarrassment. Uncle Henry looked but never said a word because he knew when she started, he would be next. Junior's face filled with pleasure as he pushed back laughter when Daddy's face went numb.

"She acts like that because of that old mean step Mama she had to stay with after her real Mama died.

Grandpa Daniel tried to help, but he had to work in the fields to put food on the table. That mean old woman just told her over and over how black and ugly she was." Daddy tried to have explained Grandma Mary's life in a nutshell.

This was a foul dysfunction that had been rooted in Grandma Mary's emotional core at an early age. A spirit that had grown and manifested into Daddy's spirit as well, and was passed on to Junior and Bree.

"Come on in and have a seat Mary. Yawl children go back out there on the porch. The others will be here in a little while. Lord knows they don't go nowhere on time." Grandpa Sidney said and lit his cigar.

Before they sat down, Junior saw the black pick-up truck as his Uncle Henry drove into the yard and parked.

"They're here. YEAH! Junior shouted.

Junior's favorite Uncle Henry, Aunt Anna Jean, and his three first cousins always joined the family for Sunday dinner although they had not attended church. Game recognized game, so Uncle Henry stayed away from Reverend Phillips shenanigans. Uncle Henry and Aunt Anna Jean were like two evil forces that had been pulled together and stuck. They stuck together like Bonnie and Clyde. Right or wrong, they had each other's back.

With a wounded soul, Bree slumped off to the front porch after her talk with Grandma Mary. Uncle

Henry and Aunt Anna spoke to Bree as she sat and sulked on the outer edge of the porch. Uncle Henry patted Junior on the back, and they smiled at each other.

Their three first cousins Henry Jr., Judson, and Barbara Mae, found a place on the porch and sat away from Bree. Junior and Henry Jr. made fun of each other. Teasing each other seemed to be the only way they knew how to have conversations. Judson looked at them and smiled. Barbara Mae played in silence with her white dolls.

Bree's mind was still dazed by her conversation with Grandma Mary. Sick of being on the porch with the others, she walked past her cousins without a word being spoken.

"Where you going, looking all crazy, gal?" Junior said, and they all laughed.

"What do you have on, anyway? That's the ugliest dress I have ever seen." Henry Jr. teased, and giggles and laughter broke out on the porch.

Bree kept walking straight to the car. She took one last look at the brown box Grandma Mary gave her, and placed it underneath the back seat. She slammed the backdoor of the car before she had realized how hard, and the sound was heard across the front yard and in the house. Daddy heard the slam and immediately jumped to his feet. From the front door of the house, he screamed at Bree.

"Get back up on this porch and sit down, before I come out there and tear your little tail up, gal."

"Oh, shut up, you old nagging fool," Junior whispered loudly in Daddy's direction. The first cousins in unison turned to see if Uncle Wallace had heard Junior's words. Apparently, he had not heard Junior, or pretended he had not heard. If he had decided to react, the front porch of the house would have become a mid-afternoon dust storm, with Junior as the tumble weed. Laughter and teasing started anew for Bree as she walked back up on the porch.

"Ah-ha, that's what you get blackie," Henry Junior chimed in. Judson found Grandpa Sydney's Checkerboard, and played Checkers alone. Bree pushed past her cousins and Junior and went back to her seat on the swing at the far end of the porch. She rocked from side to side to move herself on the porch swing. Words of the day moved to pains.

"Like son like mother." Bree made a mental note to herself.

Today the view of the apple orchard and the new puppies had changed forever.

HOME SWEET HOME

The small and shallow confines of the conventional and laid-back town of Allendale were covered with dirt roads everywhere. Some of the most gigantic trees from top to bottom housed the sweetest mouthwatering fruits Bree had ever tasted. Seasonal vegetables were always grown and ripen to the perfect taste before being harvested from the lavished and luscious gardens. Her life at an early age was spent planting, hoeing, and harvesting the vegetables in Mama's gardens. Mustard, turnips, and collard greens were the true pride of the garden, with overlapped leaves so thick and green no dirt was seen in between.

"Crop some of the mustards today, we had turnips Sunday," Mama said while the basket she carried was overran with field peas she had picked three rows over.

"Amazing grace, amazing grace, how sweet the sound that saved a wretch like me, I once was lost, but now I am found, yes Jesus," Mama's voice soothed the late fall's heat as they made their final round to the end of the rows. Their picking and cropping of vegetables were done for today. They headed to the house to have cleaned and washed the greens in cool water in the sink. Later Bree and Mama would shell the peas that filled the large wicker basket.

"All right, we are done for today. Shake that dirt off, and put the greens in the sink with some cool water. Then we are going to shell the peas while those greens soak." Mama sat the schedule for the day.

"Yes, ma'am," she knew the rest of her day was devoted to the meal they would feast on when Daddy and Junior came home from the fields.

She had deemed Mama to be the best cook in the South, although Grandma Mary had a slight edge over her on certain dishes. Mama and her sister had coined their art of cooking southern style dishes. Especially their savory sweet potato and coconut pies. Grandma Lilly's pies and jelly cakes were masterpieces fit for a king. She made them with so much rich pure butter and refined sugar, Bree's teeth seemed to hurt just from the smell of it. They never made apologies when they fried fish, chicken, pork chops, or any other meats in the same tub of lard that sat in the middle of the stove. Lard harvested from the fried fat sliced after pigs were slaughtered in the fall. Bree would hear Mama and Aunt Mamie say to each other when they tasted a dish they really liked.

"Sis, you stuck your foot in that."

The recipes were not taken from the fancy Betty Crocker Cookbooks that came in the mail as free samples, nor were they written and recorded. They were recipes Grandma Lilly had memorized and passed on to her daughters. Bree was not afforded the opportunity to have soaked up the generational knowledge of cooking because she was often ushered from the kitchen by Mama after greens had been cleaned, and peas and beans shelled.

After the greens had been picked, and the peas shelled, her help was no longer needed. She anxiously stood by the sink and tried to have grabbed peeks of how they were prepared.

"Move out the way girl, you are in the way. I need this place to work," Mama said twice.

Bree's time was limited in the kitchen, so she didn't see how meals were prepared from scratch. Mothers and grandmothers of the South were well-known for their passed-on from scratch recipes. The beautiful art of meals passed down from generation to generation that satisfied the souls of many.

When visits were made to Grandma Lilly, Bree was invited to help while she whipped up piping hot, mouthwatering peach, blueberry, and blackberry cobblers. They picked the berries during the early mornings when they were in season from the bushes and trees in nearby orchards and fields. Grandmother Lilly's cobblers were never complete without the large scoops of homemade ice cream mix she scraped from the paddles of the old fashion ice cream maker that required ice and salt. She would stand over the ice cream churn, and turned the handle with all her might until Bree would ask:

"Grandma! Grandma, can I help please, please?"

Bree pleaded.

"Yeah, come on, my little Bree, Bree. Now stand right here and turn the handle around and around. Keep turning and turning. Cause if you stop it won't come out right." Grandma Lilly gave Bree a pat on the head and returned to the kitchen to have checked the peach cobbler as it bubbled and browned in the oven.

Grandmother Lilly was her favorite to be in the kitchen with. Bree loved her long and warm hugs. She never understood why Mama was nothing like her favorite grandma, and Aunt Mamie was.

During the summer months Bree spent nights with Grandma Lilly. She always made a special effort to have something sweet for her to eat.

She relished her job, and she ensured the churn kept moving in a circular motion. The paddles of the old ice cream maker made its rotations around the wooden bucket. The cream and sugar would transform into the most delicious, delectable, luscious, and creamy sweetness that made her palate danced with uncontrollable ecstasy. The taste always left Bree delirious and giddy inside

A NASTY TASTE OF HISTORY

Beyond the plowed and planted rows of fields with massive crops laid a nasty taste of reality. A distasteful period in history that brewed and simmered each and every day of Bree's life. But like the freshly washed and bleached white sheets that hung on Mama's clothesline, and dangled freely as they danced in the wind. White sheets covered the faces of those that hung Blacks that swayed from backwoods trees.

Bree overheard conversations from white folks of the small town when they joked about Dr. Martin Luther King Jr.'s birthday being legalized.

Bree remembered one of the times she and Matthew was at the Dunbar's store, and Old Man Dunbar and Mr. Nixon were telling jokes about the holiday. She was puzzled why they laughed so hard when he said to Mr. Nixon;

"Well, John, you know if they kill four more, we can take a week off," Old Man Dunbar joked.

Mama snapped Bree's mind back to the swing when she called her and Junior to the house for supper.

"Bree, Junior, come on in here it's time to eat supper." Mama summoned them from the door of the back porch. Without a moment's hesitation, she hopped off the tire swing and raced Junior across the yard to the bottom step.

81

"I won, sucker," Junior said to Bree. Sweaty and covered with stink, they rushed to their assigned chairs at the supper table. For the first time in a long time, the family seemed to have been in a pleasant place. The conversations were usually solemn and uneventful, but tonight was different.

"Berta, you heard that white gal was killed last night down there near Flat Street in the alley?" Daddy asked mama.

"They said John Henry boy did it. But you know that old lazy boy didn't killed anybody. He's too lazy to get up off his good- for-nothing tail and do anything. That boy wouldn't hit a lick at a snake if it tried to bite him. He's about as useful as a steering wheel on one of them cows out there. I bet you that ole big tall crazy-looking white boy did it."

Daddy spoke in between bites of the lip-smacking fried pork chops with gravy and rice, stovetop brown crispy cornbread, fresh mustard greens, and peas seasoned with pork pigtails.

"Well, he's going to be put in jail even if he didn't do it," Mama said with very little concern. Daddy went on and on as he joked about John Henry Jr.

"That boy is too lazy to scratch his own behind."

Racial tensions were more pronounced when blacks were accused of crimes they had not committed. Especially in the small community where everyone knew each other. Bree saw the vicious beast of the segregated South for the entirety of her elementary school years. Allendale Elementary School, housed all the black students in the town.

Her entrance into the first grade at Allendale Elementary school began as a battle with difficult and overwhelming encounters. All the years of being teased and ridiculed by her family and folks at the church destroyed Bree's self-worth. She separated her mind, body, and spirit from her softer feminine side. Being pushed into the box, Mama and Grandma Crabby Apple had built caused Bree to have rebelled just as the white people had done when it came to their precious rights. She made herself to have looked less and less girly, and gravitated to a total tomboy look.

"I'm going to wear my overalls and blue plaid button-up shirt. The blue New York Yankees baseball cap that Mat gave me will match this nicely," she told herself while she pranced around in front of the floor-length mirror for her first day of school.

Bree had become comfortable with her new found look that was outside the box. But at school, she found her free spirit was suppressed by those around her. Not all in her presence supported the new Bree, and she constantly found herself on the wrong side of her teachers, especially her first-grade teacher Mrs. Green and Principal James.

"On your mark, get set, go," Bree shouted on the playground to the other three racers.

"Dang, we lost again," Michael said as he looked at Smokey and Sammy after the third race of the day.

Bree moved to the table behind the swing set. "Who wants to arm wrestle?"

"I do," Sammy said with a high-pitched voice.

"Come on, Bree, Bree, I can win this one."

Mrs. Green saw them and immediately walked to them with long strides.

"Bree, you and Sammy come with me right now. This is the second time this week I have told you two this was not appropriate. You can injure your arms."

Bree and Sammy were accompanied to Principal James's office. Mrs. Green made them walk in front of her in a straight line like they were going off to war. The short distance from the play ground to the main office seemed like an eternity to Bree. Mrs. Green knocked twice on Principal James's door after she was told by his secretary he was in his office.

"Good afternoon, sir. I am so sorry to interrupt you. But these two were arm wrestling again. It's the second time this week at recess I have had to speak to them.

"This child right here." She's always running around and fanning her little fast tail around those boys."

Mrs. James said and kept her eyes plastered on Bree.

"They both know it's against the school's rules. They could injure their arms or get splinters in their skin from that old wooden table," Mrs. Green explained dramatically to Principal James.

Principal James was a man of very few words because the paddle in the corner spoke for him. So he let his paddle do the talking, and Bree and Sammy's butts understood his speechless conversation.

"Go back to class and get your lessons," Principal James said emotionless after the deed of the day had been done. Bree closed the door, and saw Principal James after he had reached for the phone. She knew what the end of the day would bring after the dreaded phone call was made home. The two walked back to class in silence still angry at mean old Mrs. Green.

"She make me sick." Bree looked at Sammy with a frowned face.

"Me too. I can't stand looking at her old ugly face everyday, Sammy said as they had made it back to the class. Sammy opened the door for Bree. They entered and took their seats. Mrs. Green was explaining her daily rounds of multiplication facts to the class. She had students to stand and recite the multiplication tables one through twelve. Bree and Sammy were not in the mood to have participated after their visit with old Principal James.

"I'm going to beat you when we arm wrestle again," Bree mouthed in Sammy's direction.

Bree did not see Mrs. Green.

She heard her when she said, "Hold your hands out."

Bree saw the flat, sturdy paddle and knew this would be the second time today.

"Now, since you have so much to talk about, little girl, go up to the front of the class and say your nine times tables."

Mrs. Green was liked by most of the first graders, but Bree and Sammy stayed in trouble with her.

"Yes, ma'am, 9x1=9, 9x2=16 I mean 18." Bree tried to have counted on her fingers.

"Unless you want another round today, little girl, I suggest you go sit in that corner by yourself, and study those 9 times tables. Stop all that talking to that boy," Mrs. Green fussed at Bree as the other students looked on and snickered.

"I suggest the rest of you had better get back to your work before you receive the same." With her back turned to Mrs. Green, Bree stuck her tongue out at those that had snickered at her.

These moments occurred almost on a daily basis, Bree's first year of school. One phone call after another from Principal James after Mrs. Greens' frustrations with Bree's behavior.

Through the battles, she had gained a few victories. At the end of the year, when she had received her yearly report card from mean old Mrs. Green with the big round glasses, she pulled out a victory with most of her grades.

"Look, Mama, I got two B's, two C's, and just one D this time," she ran into the house as the backdoor slammed closed behind her. Excitedly out of breath from the long run up the driveway after the bus had dropped her and Junior off, she felt satisfied.

"Girl stop slamming that damn door," Mama screamed while she moved the broom across the kitchen floor. She knew when Mama cussed, she and Daddy had argued and fussed.

"Look, Mama, look, I did good this time!!" Her round and dark brown face was filled with proudness and excitement.

"Why are you running in here like a crazy person?"

"Look, look," she handed the report card to Mama.

"Well, it's about time you do some work down there at that school. Making us look like we didn't raise you at all."

Bree's enthusiasm was doused, and the flame that burned on the long bus ride to the house went out.

END OF AN ERA WITH A RITE TO PASSAGE

At the end of 1970, Bree was in her fifth and last year at the Allendale Elementary School. That year she spent time with the nicest teacher she had since she had started school. Mrs. Williams was so much different than Bree's previous teacher in fourth grade, Mrs. Felton. Mrs. Felton was called funky breath Felton. She was meaner than an old junkyard dog, and her matted down wig smelled just like a wet dog. Bree and Sammy were no longer the loners that were singled out and called to the front of the room. Several others were placed in the corner, or had to stand beside their desk. Old Principal James's office had a line for those that needed the real paddle, and a phone call home. Mrs. Felton made her rounds in the room.

Bree felt a sense of great relief, and looked forward to her upcoming school year. She was off to Allendale Junior High School two miles away from the elementary school.

Junior's education had ended four years earlier when Daddy told him, he was better equipped to work the fields because he stayed in Principal James's office more than he stayed in his class.

The older Junior became, the more disobedient he was with adults that told him what to do, Mama and especially Daddy. There was a genuine hate-hate relationship between the two of them.

"Boy, you aren't learning anything down there at that school. "…Daddy informed Junior one morning as they all sat at the breakfast table.

"You are making me look like a joker to these people around here. Those folks been calling here talking about you can't get on the bus anymore, and that teacher is beating you all the time. Putting you out the classroom like there is something wrong with you. I am sick and tired of that teacher and the man over the school calling here. You aren't passing anything, and they want to put you in a building at the back of the school. Well, you aren't going back. You are going to work in the backfields."

"What are you talking about, man?" Junior snapped at Daddy.

"Go upstairs and change out of those clothes, I'll be out there in the truck waiting on you."

Junior was not a fan of school, but the idea of being around Daddy all day, every day made him nauseous to his stomach. Junior jumped up from the table with a fiery rage, and before he had caught himself, he had knocked the chair over at the end of the table. Luckily for him, Daddy was out of range and had not heard the crash. Mama stood in silence with her back turned and stared out the kitchen window. Junior turned to Mama for an answer.

"What is he talking about, Ma?"

She nonchalantly said, "Do what he says."

"What do you mean, do what he said? He's a dumb old crazy man with no clue. He doesn't know anything. He never says anything that make sense. Answer me, old woman. What is he talking about?"

Junior turned on Mama in a moment of rage, and knocked his breakfast plate to the floor. He stared at the back of her pink and yellow floral bed robe. When she hadn't answered, he turned and stormed up the stairs. She continued to have pretended she was busy and re-washed the already cleaned dishes in the sink.

"You are just as crazy as he is." Junior spewed the words at Mama when he reached the middle of the stairs.

He took one step at a time until he had reached the top of the staircase. Confused and enraged, he hated the two people that were at the bottom of the stairs. His freshly pressed jeans and red plaid shirt were removed and thrown on the floor. The news sneakers, still new were flung across the bedroom so hard that the left shoe dented the wall. The old dingy white tee shirt he wore when he hung out at Uncle Henry's junkyard rested on the floor. He picked it up and forced it over his head.

"Guess this is all I'll ever be, lost and dirty for the rest of my life." Junior said to the person in the mirror.

The screened back door sounded like a gun had been

fired when Junior walked out the house and slammed it behind him. He sadly stood on the back porch, and looked lost. Daddy sat irritably at the wheel of his new Chevrolet pickup truck, tapping the steering wheel continuously with his thick fingers. Mama's heart sank to a very low and dark place as she eyed Junior on the porch.

Junior's behavior at the school had deflated Daddy's enormous ego. The reality of it all was their severed father and son relationship had ended years before this moment.

The truth be told Junior was a younger version of Daddy, but more vicious and far more dangerous than any storm that had blown on the ranch.

Somehow the years between Bree's tenth birthday and twelfth seemed to have moved slower than the water in the pond. It was as if she had become stuck in the sands of time. The time between these two years felt like life had moved slower than the sweet molasses she watched being poured from a glass jar into a bowl of flour to have made the sweet bread she loved so much.

Bree reflected on how this mixed substance was whipped and stirred until the ingredients were a thick gooey glob of dark brown, and then raked into the baking pan. The sweet smell of the dough as it rose placed Bree under a spell. Until she was called to the kitchen table once the bread had cooled enough to have been eaten. She sat with a glass of fresh milk;

Mama had gotten from the cows earlier that morning.

"Slow down, girl, chew your food and drink some of that milk before you choke." Mama lectured her lightly.

"It's so good, Mama; can I have another piece, please?" She gently asked with wide eyes. Junior must have gotten a whiff of the smell from outside. He entered the kitchen, and looked like he had not eaten in days.

"Give me a piece." Junior slung his words at Mama.

His slice was thicker than the one Bree was given. Mama placed the beautifully browned bread on a saucer. Junior nastily grabbed the bread from the saucer and stomped off upstairs to his room. They both heard the door as it slammed hard behind him. Bree looked at Mama, and she just looked away.

The summer of 1970 became a blurred memory because it arrived slowly but left quickly. Bree turned twelve in August of that year. She felt a sense of new found freedom for the first time. Mama and Daddy took her school shopping, and allowed her to have picked her own clothes for her first year at Allendale Junior High.

At the tender age of twelve, Bree's body blossomed into curves. She no longer had the flat chest she was teased about. Change for Bree was strange. And Mama made no efforts to have explained her body transformation into womanhood.

Bree knew that when Labor Day was over it was time for the new school year, and time for her to have shown off the new outfit she had picked out. She tossed and turned all night with excitement and some nervousness about her first day.

"Something light and tight like dynomite. Yeah, something light because it's still hot." Bree smiled and moved her new outfits from side to side in the giant closet.

I like this together."

Bree held up a paisley yellow and orange top, and placed a pair of white bell bottom jeans at the bottom.

"Nice." Bree was pleased with her choice.

With great care, the outfit she would make her first appearance in was laid on the chair at the foot of her bed.

The smell of breakfast downstairs was Bree's alarm clock. She jumped from the bed more excited than nervous.

Bree's first day was more electrifying than she had anticipated. The day ended with no hiccups and she cheerfully skipped to the bus for the long ride home. She and her friends talked and laughed until it was her turn to have gotten off the bus. The bus pulled to a stop at its normal place by the Pecan tree at the end of the driveway. The spot that Bree and at one time Junior had gotten on in the mornings and off in the evenings.

She rushed from her seat on the bus to the door to have gotten off. She waited for Mr. Watson to have opened the door with his old wrinkled hands to let her off. He fumbled with the knob, as Bree stood and waited. She heard rounds of laughter in the background. She thought the laughter was because Mr. Watson had struggled to have gotten the door open again.

"Ha-ha, he-he," was heard in the background. The longer Bree stood at the unopened door the louder the laughter grew.

Bree was uncertain of what had happened to have caused the upheavaled commotion on the bus. Cheryl sat next to Bree but was not aware of why the laughter had erupted either.

"Oh my goodness!" Cheryl gasped for air when she saw what the others had laughed about. She so much wanted to have told her friend what others had seen, but Bree exited the bus without a clue.

"Your pants got some nasty stuff on the back." Sherry shouted from the bus's window.

Bree stopped dead in her tracks as she regurgitated the words that buzzed in the air like bees.

"What are they talking about?" Bree stood still and twisted her body and jeans, and tried to see what others had seen.

Embarrassed from the laughter and shouts from the bus's window, she sprinted the entire length of the driveway. The door slammed behind her when she ran into the house upset and crying.

"Why are you slamming that door? Mama turned in Bree's direction."

"Are you crying? What's wrong with you now? Always something going wrong with you. What is it now?" Mama hurled more bitter words in her direction.

"Everybody started laughing at me when I was getting off the bus, they started pointing and giggling, and Sherry said I had some nasty stuff on the back of my pants. Mama, what are they talking about?" Bree turned desperately to Mama for an answer.

Bree's heartbeat could be seen through her blouse, and sweat covered her forehead.

"Turn around so I can see. Lord have mercy, Jesus," Mama said with no other explanation. "Go upstairs and take those pants and underwear off. Put them in the sink in some cold water, go ahead now," Mama said and turned back to the sink.

"What's wrong with me, am I sick?"

Mama didn't answer.

"Go ahead upstairs like I said, and put that stuff in the sink, child."

Still in shock, Bree turned and walked out of the kitchen perplexed. She walked one step at a time to the upstairs bathroom, and stood over the deep white twelve inches of the sink in the bathroom. Thoughts of what had happened a few hours ago came back and weighed heavily on her mind as she felt a sudden sickness in the pit of her tiny stomach.

Bree never grasped the important meaning of this moment to her rite of passage to womanhood. She vomited her emotions onto the already soiled and stained clothes and left them in the sink.

Tangled feelings of once again being all alone penetrated her body as she fought back tears. She decided to have called her best friend Cheryl.

"Hello, Mrs. Jones, may I please speak to Cheryl?" Bree asked the voice on the other end of the phone.

"Yes, just one moment, Cheryl, Cheryl come get the phone," Mrs. Jones said with a sweet voice.

"Hello, yes, this is Cheryl."

Bree cried tears of hysteria as she pleaded with her friend to have explained what she had experienced with such great pain. Cheryl gave Bree "the talk" her Mama had given to her two years earlier.

"Thank -you, Cheryl," Bree said as she placed the phone on its cradle. Bree stood at the window with so many thoughts and emotions running rampant through her mind. She questioned why her Mama had not told her about this? Why had she told her to talk to someone else? Bree walked from the window and opened her bedroom door. From the top of the stairs she shouted to the bottom of the stairs at Mama.

"Why couldn't you just have told me?" Bree screamed at Mama.

She walked back to her bedroom, crawled into the bed and continued to have cried.

Bree was awaken from her afternoon nap by the smells of Mama's fried chicken and cabbage. Her nose perked up to have taken in more of each smell.

"Bree come on down here, it's time for supper." Mama shouted from the bottom of the stairs.

After supper Bree went outside with Mama and Daddy, and they sat on the benches that surrounded the plants and fountain in the garden. On late fall evenings when the temperature had dropped to a level of being comfortable, they conjugated from time to time in the garden. This made them to be somewhat like they were a family. Junior never joined these little fake outings.

On this particular night as the family sat in silence, hollers were heard from the end of the driveway. The sounds grew louder and louder as an old rusty white pick-up truck with a Confederate flag that stood erected by the wind drove into their driveway.

One of the ugliest and evilest people Bree had ever seen shouted vulgar words and threw a beer bottle at them.

"You niggers better not be caught out here after dark, or we are going to kill you, and skin your hides and hang you up just like dead coons. You pack of nigger coons."

In the blink of an eye, they vanished into the dust trail they had created, and Bree realized things truly had not changed.

"We better go back in the house." Daddy said in an itchy voice.

Daddy had a look that she had only seen once before. When he told the story of why Grandma Mary was so mean after she had humiliated him at Sunday dinner. Racism reared it's ugly head on his property. Property he felt had made him different from the rest. Daddy felt violated.

He decided it was best for them to have retired in the house where he felt safe and in control. A short walk from the gardens through the foyer and they were back in the kitchen. Daddy was too nervous to sit, and he paced back and forth in the open kitchen area.

"Those are Old Man Dunbar's hateful and mean

boys.".

"But Junior be hanging with them," Bree blurted out before she had realized.

"That boy isn't nothing but a fool and, he's going to end up dead if he isn't careful. Some of these folks around here got that real hate, still. Bree's Daddy said with concern.

Mama's eyes changed to a blank stare when she heard the words, "End up dead." Junior was not a good son or brother, but he did not deserve to be hurt or killed by that foolish bunch of rednecks.

As the family had made their way back into the house, out of nowhere Junior burst into the kitchen and pushed his Daddy out the way.

"Boy have you lost your mind? Putting your hand on me like that.

"Where are you going, boy?" Daddy asked Junior.

Junior had gotten bigger and stronger. Daddy hesitated when he approached or addressed questions to him. Any and all situations were like a ticking time bomb between Junior and Daddy.

"I'll be back when I get back," Junior barked the words at Daddy, and stared at Mama with malicious eyes.

Daddy grabbed the back of Junior's dingy white t-shirt, but he pulled away with a jerk that removed

Daddy's hand. He stood toe to toe in height to him, but weighed at least fifty to sixty pounds more.

"Don't you put your hands on me old man," Junior's voice was filled with more suffering than resentment towards his father.

"Boy, you are running around here with them white boys, sassing me, you are getting way too big for your britches. You going to keep on with that mouth of yours, and I'm going to jerk a knot in your neck."

"I'm going to jerk a knot in your neck, yeah, right, whatever old man," Junior mocked Daddy's words. He exited the house, got in his white Mustang, and sped off into the night.

CHANGE IS STRANGE

From the moss-laden Oak trees along the Savannah River to the fields of white cotton and ripe peaches, Allendale was a picturesque haven of the rural South. In 1972 Bree entered Allendale-Fairfax High School. The small town saw more businesses and opportunities as they started opening up for members of the small community. The era of segregation had moved to an era of integration.

The summer of that year, Cousin Matthew flew in from California for his annual summer visit. Bree sat anxiously in the back seat of the car while she and Mama waited outside for her all-time favorite cousin's arrival. She tried so hard to have suppressed the big wide grin on her face as Matthew opened the passenger side door.

"Hi, Auntie Roberta," Matthew spoke with a whole new type of accent. The California sun had made his skin darker and changed his voice. Bree immediately noticed but kept silent.

"Where's my little Bree, Bree?" Matthew inquisitively asked, but he already knew she sat in the back because she hit the back of his seat lightly with her fist.

"Here I am, big-head," she poked her cousin in the back of his head.

"Look at you, you look so different," Matthew's

acceptance of her new appearance was very important. Her new found look astonished Mat.

"Look at you, all dark and tanned, hair all wild," she replied with a gigantic and warm smile. Mama pulled away from the front entrance of the airport and merged into oncoming traffic. Bree and Mat chattered away as the driver stayed silent.

The drive took longer today, but the cousins had not minded. Mama focused on the road and the gospel songs that played on the radio.

"I missed you guys," Mat said, sounding different than before. The accent he once had was now long gone. His accent had been crossed between the South, the North, and the West Coast.

"Yeah, right, you hardly ever called," Bree pointed out to her cousin.

"Busy little cousin, busy with classes."

"I start high school next month, you know."

"I know little cousin. Auntie I'm hungry, can't wait to taste some of your home cooking. It's been a long time since I had some of that good old fried catfish and cornbread like you cook."

The big Cadillac pulled into the canopy-covered driveway. Mama drove around to the back entrance and entered the carport attached to the back of the house. The water fountains in the garden blasted steady flows of water, and the mist hit their faces as they exited the leather seats of the car.

Matthew's eyes lit up when he saw the swing. They raced to the tire swing just like old times.

Mat had been accepted to the University of Southern California on a basketball scholarship. He embraced and loved being on the west coast, the trips to the beach with his new friends, the presence of people who had not judged or treated him differently because of his skin tone. Bree and Matthew talked for what seemed like hours under the giant Magnolia tree.

"How have things been going for you, Bree, Bree?" Matthew felt the negative energy, and was very concerned about his little cousin.

"I'm okay, I guess. Well, no, I'm not Mat. This place is a living hell," She spoke the words before she had realized. She cried out her heart to Matthew as she pushed her feet to have moved back and forth on the swing.

"Is that why you changed how you dress? You look so different, better. I like the new you," Matthew's eyes told Bree of his approval. Although he approved, he knew there was something deeper beneath the surface of her emotions.

"Mat, they treat me like a red headed stepchild. You know, like I am not even their child. Mama is meaner than a rattle snake being poked at with a stick. Always hissing and pitching a fit. And well, that old man they say is my Daddy could start an argument with an empty house. I hate Junior so much, he makes my skin crawl, always stink and dirty, smelling bad enough to gag a maggot." She began to weep.

"They act like they are all about the church and that old thing called Reverend Phillips. But they can be all Christianly when he's around and fight and cuss each other like the devil in hell. Junior tells them off and goes on his way. They turn all their anger and hate on me." Bree wept and sobbed. Matthew went over to his cousin and extended his hands to have helped her from the swing.

"My Bree, Bree, I wish I could wash away all your pain. I had no idea you were going through so much. I know Aunt Berta can be too strict sometimes, but I didn't know she was like this, and well, Uncle Wally he is a lot to handle. I can't imagine being around him all the time. Junior is a nightmare from a bad dream. He kind of stick in your throat like hair in a biscuit." Bree half heartily smiled. Mat gave her the big bear hug. She fell limp against his wide athletic chest, and looked up into his concerned eyes.

"Mat, they say things and let other people say things about my looks and my body. Especially, old dog face Reverend Phillips."

Bree changed her appearance after Reverend Phillips

started making more and more inappropriate comments on his Sunday visits to the house, and lude stares he gave from the pulpit.

"I didn't like how people looked at me, the stares and glares. So, I set my spirit free," Bree proudly pronounced to Mat.

"What are you talking about?" Mat knew, but he wanted her to answer.

The freedoms of California loosened the bonds of southern conformity Matthew had experienced being raised by Grandma Lilly.

Matthew's mother, Aunt Sarah, had passed away when he was four years old. He was raised by Grandma Lilly until he entered junior high school and moved to the north to be raised by their Aunt Mamie. After Mat left the South, he found his beliefs and outlook on life were more in tuned to those of the north. His summer visits after he had lived in the north were very refreshing for Bree as she watched and witnessed his subtle transformation.

Daddy and Junior came in from the fields and saw Matthew out by the swing with Bree. They made their way over to where the two sat in peace.

"Why do you have on those funny looking shoes and that shirt with all those crazy colors?" Junior giggled as he eyeballed his cousin. Matthew's visits to the ranch after being in the north, and then on the West

Coast, the family saw a totally new being.

"These are called sandals, and the shirt is a Dashiki," Matthew tried to have explained to his rude and culturally uneducated cousin.

"Well, whatever it is, you sure do look like a clown. I wouldn't be caught dead in that mess." Junior said and laughed.

Matthew ignored his cousin and uncle as they both looked at him strange. Daddy never really cared for him. He always kept his distance like Matthew was a stranger.

"Uh hu, boy, you look like a girl to me with all that old woolly hair on your head. People around here are not going to take well to how you are looking in that stuff." Daddy sighed loudly and walked away. "That boy is just like hemorrhoids, a pain in the butt when he comes down and a relief when he goes back up."

Matthew had grown his hair into big fluffy black cotton. The puffiness of his big fluffy afro circled his bright face that had been darkened by the sun of the west coast's heat.

"I like it, I like it a lot," Bree said out loud in an effort to have irritated her brother, but mostly Daddy.

Matthew found a place in the world where his soul was released and he was embraced by others of other cultures. Bree wanted so badly to have been like her cousin; he was her hero. Mat's openness to life, how he embraced and grew from each new experience, intrigued her.

"Mat, I wish I could come and stay with you and Aunt Mamie, she always treats me so nice when she comes down for visits. She loves to give hugs and kisses, and she tells me how much she loves me. She sends me all these nice gifts, and the latest fashions no one around here has seen. The only time I hear or feel love is when she and, of course, you are around."

They talked as they walked back from the swing. Mat and Bree were having the best time talking, when Bree's curiosity surfaced. Bree stopped at the bottom step of the back porch and looked at her cousin.

"Mat what happened to your Mama, Aunt Sarah? Mama doesn't ever talk about her when I'm around. All I know is she passed away a long time ago. Sometimes she and Daddy be whispering things about her."

"I was four when she passed away, something about being sick. Grandma never really told me. I don't remember a lot, just some vague memories of how pretty she was. You know Bree, Bree, you look a lot like her," Mat told his curious cousin.

"That's a new one. I never heard Mama or Grandma Lilly say that before. Kinda odd they never said anything about her, or her death, especially to you since she was your mom."

109

"Yeah, I guess," Mat said with a heavy thickness filled with sadness in his voice. The two walked slowly up the remaining steps of the back porch in silence with deep thoughts.

A CRY TO THE UNIVERSE: FREE MY SPIRIT

Bree lacked truthful knowledge of the real world beyond the tiny town of Allendale. Daddy only knew what he knew, and truly believed the lies he told himself to be the truth. The view between what he saw and what truly existed in the real world were to say the least, flawed and distorted.

Mat's annual visit ended, and Bree once again was in a sad place. She stood at her bedroom window and watched with great patience the freeness of the birds that flew down and perched on her windowsill. The beauty of each bird fascinated her when they preened themselves in the birdbaths in the garden. Bree marveled at their chirps and cheeps and coos, and the fluttered flapping of their wings as they flew off into the clouds.

On countless days after Mat was gone and she felt all alone, she entertained her time and mind with the uninhibitedness of the birds. She wanted to be one and the same, free. She proclaimed to the Universe.

"My soul is free. I am at one with the Universe and Mother Earth."

Bree wanted more, and opened the door that caged her soul. She deemed her spirit freed and called herself, "Birdwild."

In front of the window where birds flew free, Bree declared her freedom as well.

"Seeds are planted; they grow to the surface but die, and yet in the circle of life, the soil again will rebirth life."

Bree laid across her bed and stared at the ceiling fan. Her thoughts wandered off as she fought but failed to have stayed awoke. A dream took her deeply into a grassy pastured field where she became lost in tall, perfect blades of endless grass, and patches of fruit trees and colorful wildflowers. She saw herself vividly as she rode a beautiful majestic black stallion with its long silky mane.

A voice whispered, "It's time to get off."

"Why do I need to get off?" Bree's voice whispered back.

"This chapter of your life has ended, you are free."

The dream Bree had encountered awakened a new meaning for her life. She followed the universe's clear command, and was convinced the epiphany was what her soul had sought in order to have released her family and southern strongholds.

Bree's new-found freedom did not produce the same results she saw in her cousin. He was in a place of peace. But she found her freedom released suppressed anger, and created chaotic mayhem.

A freed spirit unbridled and uninhibited rose with flames of pain. She was labeled loopy by those that once knew her. Bree was described by her teachers at school as an oddity that danced to her own beat and colored outside the lines of life.

On Bree's first day of high school at Allendale-Fairfax High School, she noticed the landscape of students had changed dramatically. The once segregated high school mandated by law, was now pressured to integrate the only public high school in the town. White parents that once sent their prized white children to Allendale Academy realized academic and athletic scholarships to the top named universities and colleges were only available through public and not private schools. Therefore, Allendale-Fairfax High School was the only choice in the small community. Their precious private school was not seen by colleges and universities as a legitimate entity that incorporated diversity.

The landscape for teachers had changed also at the new high school. For the first time, Bree saw white faces at the front of her academic classes. Gym and vocational classes were where she saw black teachers because these were the less prestigious positions.

She was happy when she saw a familiar face behind the desk of her second block English class, Mrs. Williams. She was selected and was moved to the high school because they needed some spots filled by black teachers. She ran straight to Mrs. Williams' desk and threw her arms around her waist. Mrs. Williams was caught off guard, and before she knew it, all the others she had taught in fifth grade embraced their favorite teacher.

"Good morning, Mrs. Williams, are you our English teacher?" Bree asked enthusiastically.

"Yes, boys and girls, I am your ninth-grade English teacher," Mrs. Williams smiled at all the bright faces that surrounded her.

Bree, Cheryl, Sammy, Michael, Smokey, and Ella jumped and screamed to the top of their lungs. Mrs. Williams calmed them down because the other six black students that had moved in over the summer and ten white students in the room looked on completely puzzled.

"Take your seats, boys and girls, so we can get started," Mrs. Williams said excitedly with a big warm and gentle smile.

The classes at the high school were nicer, and with fewer students. The last block of the day was Bree's science class with Mr. Gamble, an older white man with a thin beard and hair around the edges of his head, but none on the top. He sat at his desk beyond the tables with all sorts of equipment he had already set up for labs.

"Good afternoon, boys and girls, welcome to Biology. I do hope each of you had a most interesting summer. I am Mr. Gamble, and you are stuck with me for the next four and a half months," he spoke with a rugged southern accent and stellar sophistication.

The books had hardbacks and needed to be protected. Each teacher provided brown paper bags, and time was taken to have wrapped them like Christmas presents. The school was a whole lot better than the junior high school, Bree and her friends had left three months ago. Segregation was still used but in a less obvious way. White students that migrated in from the private school were placed in the advanced classes with white teachers as their leaders. A few white teachers taught in classes that were mostly filled by black students, and some of them actually taught and cared about the black students.

Ms. Montfort, the art teacher, was one of the few white teachers that cared. She greeted each student with an affectionate smile every day. She was blessed with an overdose of high energy, very young and pretty, and extremely tall for a woman. She came from Washington, D.C., as a part of some program that trained new teachers on what integration looked like in the South.

Bree's love of painting and drawing, drew her into Ms. Montfort's web. For the first semester of her freshman year, she poured her highs, and lows into paintings. Ms. Montfort gave her the liberty to have painted her feelings and not the assigned topics. Art became Bree's favorite class because Ms. Montfort seemed to be the only one, besides her favorite cousin, that understood her. She loved the ambiance of the art room, the smell of the different paints, the brightness of sunlight as it streamed through the glass

115

roof, the sounds the miniature waterfall made that sat on her desk. A desk covered in student's paintings.

Bree loved the feel of her agony being absorbed into the many canvasses, and the taste of bitter sweetness that nourished her soul when she would paint freely. Paintings that later hung on the walls of her bedroom.

"Bree, your work is very unique. I love the rich colors you have chosen," Mrs. Montfort said after each class ended.

"I feel the passions of your work."

" Do you want to talk about what you have painted?"

"Huh, the colors you have decided to use are very powerful." Mrs. Montfort's words complimented Bree.

Bree was uncertain of what to have said because no one had ever told her anything positive before about her paintings. Other than her favorite cousin. Although most of the time he teased her, he found opportunities to have given her kudos about her undiscovered talent. Sometimes his smiles were all she needed.

"Yes, ma'am, I mean thank-you ma'am," Bree's tone was low and slow.

"Would you like to talk about your work?" Mrs. Montfort asked again.

"I just paint what I am feeling at that moment,

nothing else. That's it, Mrs. Montfort."

"Okay, Ms. Bree." Mrs. Montfort did not press the conversation any further because it was time for the bell. She knew a deeper meaning laid beneath the surface of the paint.

Bree kept quiet in her classes at the new school because she feared a trip to Mr. White's office. She had not wanted to have revisited the days of Mr. James and his friend in the corner that had done all his talking. Sammy told her that the paddle here was a lot bigger and spoke volumes louder. Although they had tried their best to have abided by the rules and stayed off the grid, Sammy found himself in trouble. He had saw the incident as innocent, but Principal White thought otherwise.

After a successful season of being undefeated, the Tigers football team ended with a State Championship. It was the season for some basketball. Sammy had become quite the athlete and popular with the cheerleaders. Bree remembered when he had made the junior varsity squad, and ran all the way to class and told her.

"Congratulations! Guess those old skinny legs are good for something." Bree teased Sammy.

One afternoon a white cheerleader, crossed the established invisible color line, and lured Sammy into a conversation in the hallway. Tammy had flirted with Sammy in their math class, the one class

117

Bree was not in. After the bell rang and class was dismissed, Tammy waited around for Sammy in the hall near the water fountain.

"Hi, Sammy are you ready for the game tonight against Barnwell High School?"

Sammy was a starting point guard, and Tammy was the junior varsity cheerleader captain.

"Yeah, I guess, we ain't lost any games yet," Sammy said to Tammy giddily.

Coach Randolph had told all the players they were not to be caught talking to girls, especially white girls. Before Sammy walked away, Assistant Principal Murdaugh appeared behind the two of them.

"Go to class, young lady. Go to class right now."

"Sammy, you come with me, boy," Mr. Murdaugh commanded them.

Sammy knew why he had to go with Mr. Murdaugh, but in his heart he felt he had done nothing wrong. Especially, since Tammy had started the conversation. There was such a great fear of interracial dating in the community when the high school went to total integration, whites patrolled blacks like they had committed a crime.

This would have been a match made in hell. Tammy's father owned the local drugstore, and old man Mr. Sammy Sr. just sat on the porch because of his disability wounds from the war, chewing and spitting tobacco juice all day.

Mr. Murdaugh was tall and seemed to be the height of one of the pine trees that grew at the back of the school. He wore a tie and pocket handkerchief that coordinated with the color of his three-piece suits. One would have thought he was the principal based on how he carried himself. He was one of few at the school that really cared and tried to be nice. Most of the white teachers had not liked integration, and a few of the black teachers hadn't either.

Blacks in the small community felt their voices were gone with integration. Students lost the role models they could have trusted and modeled after. Black teachers were a pillar of strength and respect. The integration of Allendale-Fairfax High School made black students to have felt they had to get in where they were allowed to fit in.

Mr. Murdaugh seemed to have cared more than Mr. White about the black students. He closed the door that led into his small and uncomfortable office after Sammy entered, and stood by the chair in front of his desk. "Sit down son," Mr. Murdaugh nodded his head in the direction of the chair.

Sammy sat at the edge of the oversized chair. Before he had an opportunity to have spoken, Mr. White walked into the what already seemed to be overcrowded room. He moved his short and portly body near Sammy. He smells weird, like the old dish water that had been left in the sink overnight, (pee-yew) he stinks to the high heavens Sammy thought to himself. Mr. White was the complete opposite of Mr. Murdaugh, he hated integration. He came from a private school in Hampton, South Carolina. Because of his family's ties to the community, and ownership in the leading lumber company, he was selected for the position as principal by an all-white school board.

"Son, didn't Coach Simpson talk to you boys about not talking to these girls?"

"You boys supposed to stay away from them."

Some of the teachers said you been crossing the line, boy." "This is a warning this time. But next time I'm going to suspend you from school. That means you won't be able to play basketball."

"Do you understand me?"

"We won't tolerate this kind of behavior here, you understand me, boy?" The tasteless words rolled through the stench of Mr. White's breath that smelled like burnt bacon.

Sammy made an attempt to plead his case, but Mr. Murdaugh stopped him before the first word reached his lips. "Be quiet son," Mr. Murdaugh said to Sammy with sympathy. "Go back to class, and remember our talk, boy," old Mr. White said and wobbled out the office.

GOOD TIMES: LEAVE ALL YOUR TROUBLES BEHIND

The Christmas break had come, and Bree was at the end of the first semester of her sophomore year of high school. "I can't wait to see Aunt Mamie. I'll be so happy when she gets here tomorrow!" Bree's mouth barely kept up with her excitement. She felt closer to Aunt Mamie than Mama. Aunt Mamie was the oldest and looked like Grandma Lilly with flawless dark skin, thin lips, and a very narrow nose. She was shorter and thicker than Mama, but prettier.

Over the two-week break, Bree had gotten Daddy's permission and invited some of her old and new friends over to the house. She was surprised when Daddy and Mama said it was okay.

"The only ones that can come to this house are those gals, do you understand? Not any of those old, no good for nothing boys." Daddy made it crystal clear that none of them old knotty head boys, especially Sammy, was, "Going to come into his house." He had not gotten over the incident with the chewing tobacco.

Each time the door opened that afternoon and one of her friends entered, Bree felt her energy level as it raised and reached higher to the sky. Four of her closest friends, some old and some new hung out. They watched TV and listened to Christmas music as it blasted through the speakers of the stereo system in the den. It was a crisp but sunny December

121

afternoon, and the temperature was perfect for a light sweater. They had called each other up and had decided they would dress in a color for the season. Bree and Cheryl wore red sweaters, and Ella's sweater was white with a mixture of red and green. Kathy and Susie Ann sweaters were a similar shade of green. They all wore the really big bell-bottom jeans, because they were the latest fashion craze.

Mama seemed slightly less mean since her older sister was in the kitchen, and as they say in the South, they were "burning the pots."

"Mamie, what did you put in these greens? Sis, they taste something good with these grits," Bree heard Mama when she laughed out loud at her Aunt Mamie's almost country accent.

"Berta, you know they always taste better the next day. I'm going to get me another cup of coffee, you want some?" Aunt Mamie asked her sister as they laughed and talked the morning, and most of the afternoon away in the sun lit kitchen.

This was, without a doubt, the happiest she had felt since Cousin Matthew's visit that summer. They competitively joked and jived on each other. Something they had learned from Thelma, Michael, and JJ on Good Times.

"Your mama is so stupid, she was standing by a glass wall, and climbed over it to see what was on the other side," Cheryl started the rounds of jive teasing.

"Yeah, well, your mama, is so fat when she tried to weigh on the scale, the scale said, I need your weight, not your zip code," Susie told between bouts of giggles and laughs.

Susie finally got her jive out after stopping and starting over several times because she had not stopped her laughter.

Bree went off to the kitchen and fetched more drinks and Christmas cookies while the others continued the laughter and fun.

"I like most of my classes this year, except math. I'm thinking about trying out for cheerleader in the spring," Kathy said.

The high school had made a lot of changes since their freshman year. They had added more black teachers and some of the mean white ones had left and went to the private school. The boy's junior varsity basketball team had gotten a black coach.

Bree pranced back into the room with a big grin on her face, something she had not been used to doing at the house. It was always a mood of doom and gloom. She placed the tray of sweet treats and another pot of hot chocolate on the table. The table was near the window where the decorated Christmas tree lit up the room even though it was still light outside. She hopped on the couch next to Cheryl. Ella's body continued with uncontrollable laughter. The others chimed in with more glee and high fives.

On that wonderful winter day, the Five Fabulous Friends created the fondness of unforgettable memories

JUNIOR YEAR JOURNEY

As the hazy and lazy days of, the summer of 1974, crawled to an end it seemed it had just begun. Summers in the South had a tendency to do that. Bree stayed in bed late on lazy days when she had decided to not have painted on the canvas placed on the easel.

Cousin Mat had not made his summer visit because he had accepted a job at a sports center. When her stay in bed became a bore, she pushed her way into her works of art and poetry writing. Trying so hard not to have thought about the time she and her cousin would have spent together. She stayed as far away from the family as possible, and retreated to the walls of her cocoon.

The time faded quickly.

Bree's junior year of high school started with an assembly that changed her life, for the rest of her life.

"Good morning, and welcome back students. I hope each of you had a wonderful summer, and you are now ready to get back to work."

"At the change of classes, all juniors will need to report to the gym." Principal White's voice piped through the intercom system

After first block, all juniors reported to the gym for their welcome back session. Several athletes, cheerleaders, club presidents, and the junior class

Student Council representative were among those that participated on the program. Sammy, now captain of the varsity basketball team, said the pledge of allegiance. After the pledge Principle White walked to the podium and began his boring speech. He rambled on and on for what seemed to have been forever.

He finally ended his speech with, "Now it is the time young people for you to take charge of your future. Time to think about where you are going, and what you will do to make this a better world. Will you attend college, or a trade school? What will your job of the future be? Think about it young people."

"Now our eleventh grade counselor, Mrs. Buxton is going to talk to you about some options you may not have thought about. Boys and girls ask yourself the question, where do I go from here?"

After Principal White wobbled back to his seat, Mrs. Buxton, the eleventh-grade counselor, stood at the podium in the center of the basketball court.

Mrs. Buxton was the first black counselor to have worked at Allendale-Fairfax High School. She was an older woman who had aged gracefully and dressed impeccably. She had worked as a business education teacher at the vocational school prior to being moved to the counseling department at the high school in 1972. There was something about Mrs. Buxton that reeled Bree in, like how she felt about Ms. Montfort.

Ms. Montfort left at the end of Bree's sophmore year.

The program she was a part of was some sort of government experiment that lasted for two years, and she went back to Washington, DC. The new art teacher was an "old fart" that reeked of gin and cigarettes. He glared and stared at the cheerleaders like old raunchy Reverend Phillips stared at the female members of the church, and Bree when she had gotten older.

Mrs. Buxton reminded Bree of the warmness, and the authoritative yet gentle nature of Grandma Lilly.

"Good morning, young women and young men, I am Mrs. Buxton, your eleventh-grade guidance counselor. I am here today to start the wheels in your minds turning. Yes, turning and spinning with energy to propel you into the future with success. Wheels to move you into the next phase of your life. Whether you are thinking about going off to college or to a trade school, or work, the time is upon you to get aboard the train of the future. Your future is right around the corner, on the other side of the tracks. It's that time, time for each of you to start thinking about your future, and where your place is in the world. I have an open-door policy, so you can come to my office and start exploring your options." Mrs. Buxton expressed with what Bree felt was a genuine concern for each and every one of the almost two hundred students in the gym.

She had not thought about her future up until this point. She and Cheryl sat next to each other. They gazed at each other, deep in thought.

"Wow, college, I never thought about this," Bree whispered to Cheryl.

"Me either," Cheryl whispered back with a big sigh at the end.

At the end of Mrs. Buxton's speech, Mr. Murdaugh dismissed the students to have either gone to their classes or lunch. Bree and Cheryl walked slowly to the cafeteria, grabbed their lunch, and went to their favorite bench on the side of the school underneath the old Oak tree.

Today's lunch was Bree's favorite, but she was in a different place and just picked at her corn and macaroni and cheese.

"I never thought about college before, but Mrs. Buxton made me think about it," Bree looked up from her now cold lunch, speaking more to the air than Cheryl.

Her grades were not the best, and she pondered what the grade requirements for going to college were. Her math and science classes were hit and miss. She had failed both semesters of Spanish. English and Social Studies were stronger areas, and she had carried mostly A's and B's and an occasional C. These areas gave her the outlet she loved so much, reading and studying about different places and writing poetry in the comfort of her bedroom on Saturday and Sunday afternoons. There also was no one to have helped with any of her homework. Ms. Montfort had tutored her from time to time, and it helped her pass tests.

The older she got, the more the family grew apart, especially Daddy. Mama remained in a distance place, and Daddy saw more and more of the light-skinned lady that drove the fancy new cars.

Bree remembered the wonderful and delightful Christmas time she had with her friends. And visited their homes throughout the second semester of her junior year. On these visits, she saw the unequivocal differences between a house and a home. She saw her friends' families as they hugged each other, and expressed their true feelings. They talked and laughed about their day, and enjoyed healthy and normal relationships. They were wrapped in the goodness of living happy lives.

"My mom is having a birthday get together for me on Saturday," Kathy announced to her friends as they sat at the long lunch table near the window in the lunchroom filled with students. Kathy's birthday was March 3rd.

"I want yawl to come, okay?

The boys that sat at the table behind her overheard the conversation and butted in without being invited.

 "We want to come," Sammy and Michael said at the same time. Bree's heart almost left her chest.

"I was going to tell you, if you just shut-up and let me finish, dang. So rude," Kathy snapped at Sammy.

"Okay, girl, you ain't got to be so mean, dang." Michael said sarcastically as he and the others giggled at the girls.

"Yawl can come, my Mama said, but no dancing slow together," Kathy made sure they understood. Bree's heart skipped another beat at that point.

"Are you going to let those boys come to your party, Kat, at your house?" Bree was shocked to have heard these words from her friend.

"Yeah, she said it's okay Bree. My parents said its fine," Kathy said with a slight hint of irritation and puzzled look at Bree's concern.

Bree's mind thought back to Daddy's words.

"No boys going to come in my house, especially that boy name Sammy."

She wondered why Daddy was so unyielding when it came to boys, and especially Sammy.

"Didn't your Mama talk to you about the talk or what mine called the birds and bees after we talked that day?" Cheryl asked her closest friend.

Bree sat in silence and thought back on the day she hysterically ran into the house with tear stains on her face and bloodstains on the back of her pants. She remembered when Mama told her to have asked

Cheryl about this.

Bree wondered what had she missed beyond "the talk"? What was the so call most important life or death talk.

"Michael is s-o-o-o-o cute. I hope he comes to the party," Ella said out loud as she flirted with him.

"I'll be there with bells on," Sammy said while he flirted back and winked at Bree.

The behavior was very foreign to Bree, and she frowned with uneasiness, although just a tiny bit intrigued.

At supper that night she asked Mama and Daddy about the party. She inadvertently left out the part about boys.

"Um, Kathy's parents are having a birthday get together Saturday, and I was wondering if I can go?" She stumbled with her words as she crossed and uncrossed her fingers. Bree made a final cross of her fingers for luck because she knew she had not told the whole truth.

"Listen here, you can go over there to Leroy and Johnnie Ruth's house, but they better not call here talking about anything crazy you've done over there, you understand me, girl?"

Daddy gave his previous usual staled speech and sounded like some old jail keeper. Mama just looked without any reactions or words. They were allowing her to go, and nothing else really mattered. She tuned them both out and thought of how this was her first party with boys, and about what she was going to wear. Although she was a junior, she had not had boys paid her any attention in a way other than just being one of the guys.

Bree wondered deep in her mind what Ella felt when she flirted with Michael.

After Bree calmed down when she was told she could have gone to the party, images ran through her mind of Michael, and Sammy and some of the other boys in her classes. Mama and Daddy had placed so much fear of boys in her mind.

"Gal, you know if you look at a boy too hard, you are going to end up being around here with a child on your hip," she remembered Daddy had said after the incident at Mr. Sammy and Mrs. Fannie Mae's house. The words had been pushed into a suppressed place. A place she had hoped that they would never have resurfaced. But now they stood at attention in the front part of her mind.

"It's party time, time to party," she pranced and danced in front of the huge floor length mirror in her bedroom. She had decided to have worn her hair in a gigantic afro puff that surrounded the top of her head. The girls had decided they were going to rock similar looks again. Since it was close to spring, they wore different pastel colors. Yellow was her energy color and perfect for the party. She matched her yellow long sleeve flared blouse with freshly pressed bell-bottom jeans and a pastel-colored head wrap. As hard as she had tried, nervousness still filled the pit of her stomach and outweighed the vibes of excitement that ran through the rest of her body. She slid on her sandals when she heard Mama at the bottom of the stairs.

"Let's go, girl, come on here."

"I have got stuff to do today."

"I have got to get back and cook these beans for dinner after church tomorrow."

They rode in silence for the first ten minutes of the fifteen-minute ride. The words of Daddy rode with them like another passenger in the car. She had hoped Mama would have cleared up some of these weird feelings before they had reached the pathway that led to the house. Maybe even a gesture to tell her she looked pretty for the party. She searched for a mother moment but only felt the presence of Mama. Bree horded feelings of being lost, not loved, and not connected to the woman she sat beside on the fifteen minute ride.

Kathy's parents lived in a sub-community to the south of Allendale called Fairfax. Their home was built not far from the road Bree's Mama had turned onto from the main road. Their home always felt warm and cozy when Bree visited because Kathy's parents were the complete opposite in every aspect of hers.

Mama parked the car at the end of the arched walkway that led to the front porch of the house. She generally dropped Bree off here but decided today to have gone in and spoken to Mrs. Johnnie Ruth since she had not seen her in church for a while. Bree's heart pumped in her chest so fast she knew for sure she would have had a heart attack.

"Mama! Where are you going?" She squeezed out the words, and her eyes looked like a deer that had been caught in the headlights of an eighteen-wheeler.

"Come on here, girl. I'm just going in to speak to Johnnie Ruth and to see how Deacon Leroy is doing." She said as she took long strides to the porch with the white wicker chairs and matching table.

Everyone Kathy had invited was already there and sat in various places throughout the fuzzy and cozy house. Bree lagged behind Mama with knots tied in the pit of her empty stomach. She waited at the front door before she knocked and entered the house to have given Bree an opportunity to have caught up and entered first.

"Hi Bree, Mrs. Breeze. How are you all doing today?" Kathy asked.

"Come on in, my mom is in the kitchen, Mrs. Breeze."

"Mom, Mrs. Breeze, and Bree are here." Kathy smiled and pointed her voice in the direction of the kitchen.

"Yawl come on in Berta. These children got me busier than a cat in a room full of rocking chairs," Mrs. Johnnie Ruth said and continued to spread the icing with the spatula on the cake she had baked for Kathy's seventeenth birthday. The icing looked so enticing to Bree on the cake as Mrs. Johnnie Ruth swirled and smooth the sides and top of the cake with the precision of a professional baker. The moment was short-lived when Mama burst into laughter and reminded her she was still there.

"Bree go ahead in the front room with the others," Mrs. Johnnie Ruth steered her out of the kitchen with her words and hands.

"Hi Bree, you look really pretty. I love your yellow blouse," Ella said as she ran and gave Bree a Grandmother Lilly hug.

"Yeah, right looking like a black banana in all that yellow," Smokey said out loud, and the entire room laughed uncontrollably.

Bree was already in a panicked place but gave a half smile. Just as the laughter subsided, Mama came from the kitchen and looked like a bat that had flown out of hell. She looked around the room and saw Sammy on the arm of the couch, and the other boys scattered around the room.

"Uh-uh, Lord, have mercy."

"Look at this. I can't believe these children are all over Leroy and Johnnie Ruth house like this." "Jesus, Jesus, what is this world coming to?" Mama mumbled as she stared out into the sea of faces. Bree looked down at the floor and hoped it would have some how absorbed her.

"Come here, girl, get over here right now," Mama threw the words at her like darts and they hit her like she was the bull's eye. The room grind to a halt and the only sounds came from the music that blasted from the back porch.

"Oooh, you are in trouble," Smokey said with his evil laugh.

"Shut-up. Just shut-up Smokey," Cheryl barked.

Bree knew that even in Mama's greatest moments of craziness, she always had another level of insanity.

"Lord, Jesus child, you knew those old rusty behind boys were going to be here, didn't you?" Her eyes looked like those of a Tasmanian Devil as she threw the words in the room.

"Get your little fast tail in here right now before I slap the black off of you."

She walked past Mama, entered the kitchen, and stood near the cake Mrs. Johnnie Ruth had worked so hard on. Bree feared for her safety. She had hoped the cake would have been her savior.

"Lord, Jesus." Mama's said.

The onlookers looked towards the kitchen in awe. They were not clear as to why Bree's crazy Mama had caused such a ruckus on a happy occasion.

"What's wrong with that old cuckoo lady?" A muffled voice said low, but against the silence, it seemed loud. The music had stopped, and the DJ peeked from around the China Cabinet that housed the fancy dishes.

"Get your little tail in that car, and don't you say a word," the old witch shouted with a high-pitched voice.

Bree felt like she had felt the day in first grade when she walked back to her seat in front of the entire class, but this time the scene was on steroids. Her steps from the couch in the living room to the kitchen felt like the walk of shame as she walked pass all her friends. Some were concerned, and others held their mouths to have concealed their laughter.

The fifteen minute ride back to the ranch seemed like an infinity. The fussing from Mama buzzed inside the car like someone had knocked down a hornets' nest. At the age of sixteen, she was still called child and girl by Mama, just as if she was still six.

"Girl, you thought you was slick didn't you?

"When your Daddy asked you about them boys, and you sat right there at that table and said nothing."

"You must think we are dumb as a bag of rocks?"

"I can tell you this; you won't be able to sit down on that little fast tail of yours when that old man gets done with you."

"You make me sick to my stomach, you just keep making us a shame like this," Mama said with enough force that it shook the front window of the car.

The conversation for Bree was dead. She fixated her mind on the view from the side of the car and tuned Mama out.

"Old lady, I'm going to change the channel on this station. I'll deal with what I need to deal with when we get back." Bree's thoughts remained inside her head.

Bree was not to certain how she was going to have faced her friends at school on Monday. They looked so terrified of Mama when she entered the living room, except the boys that laughed. Sammy was not one of the boys that laughed but seemed to have felt compassion for his friend and partner in crime.

Her eyes welled up with tears, and the streams flowed down her face and puddled at the bottom of her chin. Mama continued to yap and yap about how she had lied.

Bree turned in Mama's direction and asked in a low tone, "Why, why did you do that?" Mama continued her outburst of angry energy and chatted over Bree's words and broken emotions.

Her voice changed from low to high like a race car headed to the finish line.

"I said, why would you do that, Mama? Why did you do that in front of all my friends?" She questioned Mama between tears and sobs.

"You sat right there and lied. I knew you weren't telling the whole truth at the table the other night. Sitting there fidgeting around in that chair, hands moving back and forth. That's why I went in the house with you instead of just dropping you off. You ain't grown. Until you are grown and gone, child, you are going to follow the rules in this house. Next thing you know you'll be around here a child with a child on your hip."

"How am I going to get a child, Mama?" Bree shouted.

But before an answer was exchanged, the car turned into the driveway, drove into the carport, and parked.

"Don't you raise your voice at me, girl. I'll slap you clear into the middle of next week. Get on in that house. Acting like some old loose jezebel woman, running behind them stink behind boys."

"What are you talking about? This is so stupid. You make me sick," Bree garbled and slammed the car door with all the energy and force she had left.

Any other time Daddy would have been gone on a Saturday afternoon, but he sat in the den with the TV up louder than normal.

"Berta, is that you? What are yawl doing back here so soon? I thought you were going to wait over there until they were through."

"Come on in here, gal, get in that kitchen, and sit your little narrow tale in that chair." Mama said and frowned at Bree.

"No, we are back early."

"This child lied to you."

"She didn't say anything about them boys that were there."

"I knew she was lying when she asked because she couldn't sit her little fresh tail still."

"When I went inside to speak to Deacon Leroy and Johnnie Ruth, I saw a bunch of them old disrespectful boys sitting up there like they owned the house."

"Got on my last nerve, especially that old touched in the head boy of Sammy's."

"Girl, what's wrong with you? You touched in the head too? I have told you over and over about being around them, boys. Lord only knows, you are going to be the death of me. If it ain't that old nuttier than a fruit cake brother of yours doing something stupid, it's you. Well, I am going to show you better than I can tell you what I mean about staying away from them boys, gal." Daddy and Mama looked at each other and shook their heads at the same time.

She sat in angry silence because she knew no answer she gave would have mattered.

"I keep saying the same thing over and over to you, and you keep being hard-headed. You keep running behind them good for nothing boys, you going to end up with your life ruined. That's all a child on your hip will do. I am going to show you how a hard head makes for a soft tail."

"Why do they keep repeating that old dumb saying over and over?" Bree's eyes darted from Daddy to Mama with questions she needed answered. But she never spoke out loud.

Junior walked in and slammed the back door. Without a word, he walked past the commotion in the kitchen, and sprinted up the stairs.

"Boy, where have you been?" Daddy shouted with an already hot irritation in his voice.

Junior ignored them all, continued to his bedroom and slammed the door. Bree's mouth cracked a semi-smile for a quick second because Daddy's face shifted to another level of frustration and agony. He picked his battles because he knew the quickest battle to have won was with Bree. He had lost the war years ago with his son.

Daddy gathered his composure after being fueled with anger and fire, lifted his body from the chair and stood at the kitchen table. They all knew what was next because it had been done so many times before. Mama started the beans she talked about earlier. She slammed and shuffled pots and pans from the cabinets to the stove.

"Go ahead up the stairs to your bedroom," Daddy ordered.

Daddy climbed the stairs. Bree hesitated on the stairs but felt Daddy's presence behind her. They entered the room gently, but the storm quickly struck. The sounds beyond the door made Mama's skin crawled, but she busied herself to camouflage the echoes of Bree's cries. He emerged shortly after the storm had passed, walked through the backdoor, and disappeared into the dust fall of the evening.

Junior had heard the turmoil from his room, and the anger he already had, grew even more. He knew too well what had just happened. He walked pass his sister's bedroom and glanced at her as she sat with her back to the door and looked past the scenery beyond the window. He shook his head in disgust when he walked pass Mama in the kitchen, once again with her back turned.

"You are something else, or should I say, nothing else. You make my blood boil." Junior threw the words at his Mama's turned back like sharp daggers.

Blinded by the thickness of all this, Bree stumbled and groped in the darkness of her inner being. She tried to have understood what had happened in the last four hours of her life. Why was it that her friends, were allowed to be around boys, and she was held to such a different standard? Why was the need so great to have kept them away?

"What are they talking about?"

The events of her first party at sixteen with her friends and boys were entangled into a day of embarrassing devastation, and heartbreak. She screamed at the universe that sat beyond the window she faced, and pleaded for release from her pain. The last three months of her junior year were a daily nightmare on earth. The boys teased her and mocked the words Mama had spewed in the kitchen as Mrs. Johnnie Ruth looked on in shock.

"Bree, Bree pants on fire, your momma spanked you and now you are a crier. Man, I sure wouldn't want her for my mama, she C-r-a-z-y as a soup sandwich. When you left, we all laughed and hollered," Smokey said and started the chant in the lunchroom the Monday after the party. He chanted, "Bree's Mama is C-r-a-z-y, C-r-a-z-y like a s-o-u-p san-d-witch, nuttier than a twenty-pound fruit ca-ke, rocked Mrs.

Johnnie's house like a point five earth-quake. C-r-a-z-y, C-r-a-z-y like a s-o-u-p san-d-witch, nuttier than a twenty-y pound fruit ca-ke, rocked Mrs. Johnnie's house like a point five earth-quake." Smokey never cared much for Bree and her family. He said they were all uppity, and thought they were white.

The entire lunchroom burst into a frenzy of laughter, and the incident left Bree humiliated. Smokey always went too far with teasing, but today was more than his usual dose. "Yea, and you looked like a burnt black banana in all that yellow when you ran out the door behind your old crazy fat Mama shaking like a jelly roll." The lunchroom broke out with another rumbustious round of laughter. Cheryl angrily walked over and kicked Smokey.

"You got the nerve to talk. Ella said your breath smelled like a chicken coop when you tried to kiss her, pee-yoo. Your whole body funky and stink with your dirty self." Before Cheryl said another word, Assistant Principal Murdaugh walked in the double doors at the entrance of the lunchroom. He was too far away to have known what had happened at the back of the lunchroom. Cheryl got a couple more kicks in to Smokey's feet and a really big one to his left ankle. Bree smiled at her friend, turned and finished her favorite lunch of macaroni and cheese, corn, and the imitation Salisbury steak with thick brown gravy. Revenge felt and tasted good today.

COLLEGE CONFUSION

It was near the end of the semester, and Mrs. Buxton had been scheduling appointments with all the juniors to have discussed their plans for the future. Bree waited patiently in the outer office of the counseling department while seniors, juniors, sophomores, and a few freshmen students moved in and out of the appropriate offices.

"Hello Bree. How are you doing today," Mrs. Buxton greeted her with a handshake and a smile of gold. "Have a seat, young lady," She pointed in the direction of the chair by the window.

"I'm good," Bree said nervously. Mrs. Buxton opened the folder that sat in the middle of stacks of papers on both sides of her desk.

"Well, Ms. Bree, it's time for you to start looking at your future. You know graduation is just around the corner for you. Have you given any thoughts to whether you want to attend college, and where, or trade school, the military, or work?"

"Oh my," Bree said in her mind. She was not ready for this conversation.

A sheet that contained grades from the past three years became the center of attention. "Your vocational courses grades are all A's and B's, which is great." Bree sat up in her chair and gave a slight, quick smile as Mrs. Buxton continued.

145

"But." Again Bree spoke in her head.

"Here we go, I knew it sounded too good to be true.

"But you seemed to have struggled a great deal in your math and science courses."

"Yes ma'am, they were hard to understand sometimes."

"Now, overall, your grade point average could possibly get you accepted at some of our colleges here in the state. You will need to make sure you pick up some classes that will increase your grade point average, and no more F's. These F's drop your average really quickly. Okay, young lady?" Mrs. Buxton said all of this without taking a breath.

"Yes, ma'am," Bree's body felt a twinge of excitement and relief.

"Take these pamphlets home and show them to your parents. We will talk again at the beginning of the new school year, your last year, young lady. Are you excited?"

"Yes, ma'am, a little, I guess."

The excitement lasted only for a brief moment. As she walked slowly back to class, she thumbed through the pamphlets. Her mind was cluttered with what was said and how to have made the right decision about a college. She never thought college would have been a part of her life. The reality of life had just gotten real.

The last summer of high school had come and gone without a visit from her Cousin Matthew, again. He had started a new job and was not allowed time off. She wished her cousin would have visited so he could have advised her on college since he had graduated in the spring semester. The week before the final year of high school started, Bree decided to have talked to her parents about college, and to have shown them the pamphlets Mrs. Buxton gave her at the end of her junior year three months earlier.

"What are you talking about?" Daddy asked half listening and chopping his teeth into the fried pork chop he had just stuffed in his mouth.

"Last year, Mrs. Buxton, the school counselor, told me I could go to college because my grades are pretty good."

"College, what are you rambling about? You ain't said nothing about going to school, and how much is that going to cost?" Daddy threw out question after question in her direction.

"I don't know yet. She is going to talk to me when I get back next week. She heard Mama as she sucked in and blew out a deep sigh at the sink.

"Uh huh. Well, we'll see," Daddy said as he placed the last piece of homemade biscuit in his mouth and reached for his glass of chilled ice tea with a lemon wedge.

"Welcome Back class of 1976." Old pasty and crusty, Mr. White stood at the entrance of the gym and greeted students with his fake smile and handshake. Bree felt a sudden twinge of panic and unsettledness when he grabbed at her right hand. She returned a smile but avoided his handshake. The crew she had hung tight with was seated at the far end of the bleachers in their usual spot they had occupied for the past three years. The senior's assembly lasted for the entire first period, and she had missed her favorite art class. The one class that throughout her high school years had given her the ability to have poured her emotions into her paintings, and had developed her artistic talents. Paintings and drawings that had won several art contests and three of her paintings were displayed in the foyer of the school. She had an unusual abstract piece placed on display at the Allendale County Bank.

Mr. White highlighted several students and their accomplishments since their freshman year. Bree was one of the honorees.

"This young lady has demonstrated her ability to have created great art since her freshman year. She was also recognized by the local area college as a new and upcoming artist in the community, Bree Breeze," Mr. White said and asked her to stand.

For a second, she felt a temporary moment of

greatness when the entire gym applauded her. She saw the pride in Mrs. Buxton's face after she took her seat. A pride she wished she could have seen in Mama's face.

"Great job Bree I'm so proud of you, my friend," Cheryl said while she held on and hugged her tightly.

The assembly ended, and the students proceeded to their second-period classes. Bree and Cheryl walked with their arms locked together. Laughing and reliving the last moments of the assembly. They walked to the Guidance Office because Bree had a scheduled appointment.

"Where is my appointment card?" Cheryl asked Bree.

Here it is. I got to go Cheryl. See you at lunch." Bree waved bye-bye.

"Bye." Cheryl said to Bree.

Bree entered the Guidance Office with a smile. Mrs. Patterson, Mrs. Buxton's faithful and dedicated secretary smiled and reassured Bree she was welcomed.

"Good morning, young lady, how are you doing? Congratulations on your art recognition today in the gym." Mrs. Patterson said to Bree.

"Thank-you, Mrs. Patterson. Bree said and smiled irrepressibly.

"Hello again Bree. Great job today. I am very proud of you." Mrs. Buxton said, walked over and wrapped her arms around Bree. "Your work really is magnificent. Congratulations! Now are you ready for some great news?

"Yes, ma'am I am!

"Well, you know I work over the summer here at the school. Some of us work all year. I took it upon myself, and sent some of your work to colleges I knew with art programs. Actually, let me back up. I'm putting the cart before the horse. Did you show your parents the pamphlets, and talk with them about going to college?" Mrs. Buxton stopped in order to have given Bree a chance to have gotten some words into the conversation.

"Yes, ma'am, I did. My Daddy wanted to know what the cost for me would be. And well, that was about all he said."

"Did you study the brochures I gave you? And did any of them appeal to your interest? You know any that you would consider applying to for entrance in the fall?"

"I liked a few, but I was not sure if my grades were good enough," she became nervous again.

"I got a few more I looked up for you, especially with your accomplishments in art, and I found a school here in South Carolina that you might like. Like a lot!"

Bree's eyes lit up like a Christmas tree, and the nervousness she had felt left her body. She sat up straighter in her seat and leaned forward.

"Yes, Ms. Bree, South Carolina State College has an amazing four-year art program, and your grade point average is actually slightly above what they are requiring."

"Really, Mrs. Buxton, really?" Her excitement became obvious to Mrs. Buxton, as she placed her arms around Bree and gave her another great big bear hug. The hug caught her off guard, and before she had realized it, she had hugged Mrs. Buxton back. She felt the warmth she experienced when she had hugged Grandma Lilly. A safe and protected feeling that finally, someone else at school cared about her other than Ms. Montfort.

Outside the doors of the counseling office, a giant sigh of relief was exhaled. At that moment a place of peace in the middle of all the storms had been found. A sudden burst of energy released and relieved her pains and burdens. Anger that had been carried from home to school dispersed.

Bree skipped her lunch and conversations with her friends and sat in isolation on the bench beneath the Oak tree. The beauty of the skies seemed brighter because her soul was lighter

Bree's final year of high school brought the changes she had cried to the universe for. The once skinny

151

little tomboy that arm-wrestled and ran foot races with Sammy, Smokey, Michael, and the others had grown into a beautiful young lady. Bree"Birdwild" Breeze had come full circle. Painting became her ticket to freedom from the house. Mama stopped straightening her thick and fluffy afro. Cheryl was her only true friend because she remained with her through the ups and downs of her journey from elementary to high school. The others had the tendency to have changed just like the weather. Cheryl continued to have protected her best friend because she knew better than anyone what happened behind the walls of the Breeze house. Ella, Kathy, and Susie became more and more involved with boys. And then Ella found out she would have a child on her hip come spring.

"I wanted something different, you know. You should see the dress my Aunt Mamie sent in the mail, Cheryl. It is b-e-a-u-t-if-u-l!!"

"Why didn't your Mama help you with your dress?"

"She said she didn't have time for that."

"Oh, okay. My Mom had Mrs. Johnnie Ruth to make mine. She did a good job. I really like the style.

"I bet you will look marvelous my dear!"

Who are you going with, Bree, Bree?"

Silence covered the conversation like a wet blanket thrown on a fire. Then Cheryl remembered her conversations with Bree, about how her parents felt about boys, especially Sammy. She recognized the obvious mistake she had made, and quickly changed the subject.

"I bet your dress is really nice, and you are going to look like Diana Ross when she's singing, 'Ain't no mountain high enough.' If you need me, call me, no matter where you are, you never too far." Cheryl playfully sang the words to her friend. "With all that hair, you are going to be strutting that gorgeous gown your aunt sent, just like Diana Ross."

They continued to chat loudly and laugh about the prom.

"Bye, Bree, Bree."

"Bye, Cheryl."

Daddy decided to let her go to her senior prom, but she was still not allowed to have taken a date or be alone with none of those "old no good for nothing boys." She knew, and that was why she had not asked. Daddy's adamant words reminded her every time the conversation about the prom was brought up.

The night of the prom had finally arrived, and Bree decended the staircase at the house. Mama stood alone in the kitchen.

"You better not come back here all hours of the night.

Like some old woman of the streets. Mama said and continued to have swept the kitchen floor.

"Yes, ma'am." Bree's excitement out weighed the heaviness of Mama's words.

Beep, beep!

Bree ran to the front door when she heard the car horn. She rode with Cheryl and Michael.

She entered the gym alone and looked like an African princess in her yellow floor length gown trimmed in tiny beads of sequence.

"Look at us, Bree, looking all good," Cheryl said as they stepped into the magically decorated gym. A balloon arrangement was arched across the entrance, molded and shaped into the numbers 1976.

Bree watched Cheryl and Michael and others with dates as they danced beneath the fake stars and full moon that decorated and covered every inch of the gymnasium.

The popularity she had gained through her art and poetry writing in classes, and natural beauty she had grown into, won her prom queen, and Sammy won prom king. The school's tradition was for the crowned king and queen to have one dance. The dj played "Always and Forever," one of Bree's all-time favorites. She danced to it often in front of the mirror. But now she stood in the middle of the gym, as the lights surrounded her and Sammy, unprepared for her first dance with a boy.

"Come on, Bree, Bree, let's show them what we got, girl," Sammy said as he smiled and laughed his infectious laugh.

He extended his right hand to his life-long friend. She felt the pang of panic. It was supposed to had been a slow waltz, but the old big black Cadillac Reverend Phillips drove could have driven between them and not have touched either.

"Girl, stop being scared," Sammy said as he gently pulled his friend into his arms. She looked up into his eyes, and for the first time, saw his heart. The song ended, and she sighed with relief.

"Thank- you for the dance, my lady. Very nice, my friend," Sammy said.

The photographer for the yearbook ushered them to the side and bombarded them with pictures. The dj picked the beat up and played "Love Train" by the Ojays. She danced the remainder of the night away under the fake moon and stars with her real and forever friend, Sammy.

The bus stopped, and Bree got off at the same place she had since their move to the house.

"Bye, Cheryl, see you tomorrow!" Bree yelled to her best friend from the aisle of the bus.

"See you tomorrow."

She got off and grabbed the mail from the oversized mailbox surrounded with flowers at the end of the driveway.

"A letter for me, and it's from South Carolina State College." She ripped the back of the letter with a wild exhilaration, and she read it out loud to the universe.

"I am pleased to inform you that you have been accepted into the Liberal Arts and Science Program for the fall nineteen seventy-six semester.

I'm in. I did it. I did it!"

The news was more than she could have contained, and she jumped up and down to have celebrated her acceptance.

"Oops!" Bree said as she picked up the mail she had dropped on the ground and her literature book. Today she ran the entire length of the driveway, and continued to run up the steps of the back porch and into the house.

"I'm in. I did it. I did it, Mama, I 'm in!! I am going to South Carolina State College. I got accepted. Look, I just got the letter!"

Mama, for a change, was in the den, and not in the kitchen's window. She had just watched her last soap opera of the day, General Hospital.

"What are you screaming like that for, and slamming that door?" Mama questioned while she used her middle finger to have pushed her glasses back up on her nose.

"I did it, Mama. I did it. Look! I got in, and I get to go to South Carolina State. Mrs. Buxton helped me, and I'm going to college, Mama." Bree jumped up and down, and her hair seemed to dance to its own beat as it moved up and down around her face.

"Mama look, look, I just got the letter out the mailbox. Are you happy?" She looked to her for some level of the excitement she felt. Just a pinch of joy, a small pinch like the small pinch of sugar she had used to season the turnips she cooked so perfectly each and every time. She was surprised when she responded.

"You did good. I'm happy."

In a certain way, Mama was relieved that Bree would leave the ranch and all the stuff that took place behind the walls. She had kept her face turned away from the horror and pain Bree and Junior had suffered. Mama saw without looking, their broken spirits every time they left and re-entered the house. And she had done nothing to have shielded them from the injuries from their father.

"Thank you, Lord, thank you, my heavenly Father, for all your mercy and favor over this child." Mama prayed a silent prayer.

FLYING THE COOP

Bree entered the kitchen with her hair still tied up in a scarf. Mama had insisted that she let her straighten her hair for this occasion. No defiance this time, no fighting the waves. Bree simply rode with the flow. Mama was calmer as she laid each section of her hair gently into its proper place. On that special day, their conversation in front of the heated stove was different. Mama tried desperately to have imparted some words of wisdom, but struggled with her thoughts. The right words she needed never came because she found herself fighting back tears. Sniffles came each time she reached to the stove for the hot comb.

"Are you okay?"

"Yes, I'm fine." Sniff "I want you to do your best, and the rest will fall into place. You are a good child with a lot of smarts that got you into that school. You will do good once you leave here. I want you to stay out of trouble and study hard. Stay away from them old stink tailed boys. They don't mean you any good. Believe me, child I know all too well."

"Yes, ma'am, I will. I want you to be proud of me," Bree said as she too held back tears.

With pep in her step, Bree left the kitchen and bounced up the stairs. Her spirit and hair flowed in the air. Mama had used less grease today. Mid-way up the stairs, she turned and returned to the kitchen.

159

"I forgot to say thank-you to Mama." Their eyes met.

"Thank you Mama!"

"You are welcome, Bree." Mama said with a smile.

The morning Bree had anticipated had finally arrived.

Bree's excitement had awakened her long before Mama screamed up the stairs.

"Time for ya'll to eat! Breakfast is on the table. These eggs are going to take legs soon, and get up and walk off this table." Mama tried but failed miserably to have told a joke.

Bree smiled because she realized Mama was in a somewhat happy place. The smells of her breakfast feast that filled the house were everyone's alarm clock. She had cooked a breakfast filled with what one could have taken for love, if you looked from the outside in. The breakfast was a token of a celebration without it truly being deemed that.

"Yes ma'am, breakfast sure smells good," Bree complimented Mama and smiled. She hummed as she stirred and added water to the creamy grits on the stove that bubbled with delight. The old battered coffee pot perked and brewed to a harmonious beat next to the piping hot gravy that simmered beneath the six pieces of sausage links.

"Where is Junior at?" Daddy at the end of the table

said but truly could have cared less.

Without an answer, he yelled in the direction of the stairs. "Junior, it's time to eat boy, we are ready to eat, waiting on your sorry butt."

He then focused his attention on Bree.

"Well, girl, I didn't think I would see this day. The day you would be going off to school. I have already paid the money. I sent those people a check two weeks ago. Junior, get your butt in here, boy. And gal, you better not be up there at that school acting like you was raised in a barn. You know sometimes you do some foolish things."

"Yes sir," she said with a frown.

"Go ahead and eat, forget about that boy. We need to get on the road so your Mama and me can get back here before dark. It's deer season, and they are bad this time of the year about running in the road. End up hitting one of them and messing up the car."

Junior stumbled into the kitchen and sat in his assigned seat opposite his sister. He had slept in his clothes, and they looked like the wrinkled sheets that came out of the washing machine before Mama hung them on the clothesline. Mama sat a plate of her delectably fried sweet potatoes sprinkled with a hint of salt near the center of the table as Junior plopped down noisily. Daddy just looked at Junior and shook his head frustrated at what he saw. Bree's acceptance into college gave him some hope, but not the same hope he had for his son. Junior stared around the table at faces he felt disconnected from.

"I don't know why ya'll are acting like dummy did something, she's still stupid, and yawl are stupid too," Junior said and looked intently into his sister's eyes. He grabbed two pieces of the thick bacon and two biscuits as he pushed his chair back from the table. He fled to the backdoor, and with a quick turn in the direction of the table, turned up his nose and frowned. Junior had no desire to have participated in this charade of a send-off for his sister. Their sister and brother relationship had grown even more bitter over the years. The bitterness was sour and foul. After Daddy found out she was going to go to college, he took it as his new bragging point. This made Junior hate the house and people in it even more.

"That boy ain't worth two nickels rubbed together. I tell you what, he is going to keep on with that big fat nasty mouth of his, and I'm going to skin his hide and nail it to the door," Daddy angrily ended the conversation and picked up the bowl with the hot grits. He scooped three-spoon fulls into a pile on his plate. They ate the scrumptious meal in silence after Junior had left the kitchen in his usual rage. Bree hurriedly gobbled up and cleaned every crumb of food from her plate. She wanted seconds but knew Daddy would have had a fit if she even had thought about asking.

"All right, it's time to get a move on. Go ahead and get ready, so I can put these miles behind me," Daddy's voice said calmly, although he had been fueled with so much anger just minutes earlier.

After the table was cleared, Mama washed and dried the dishes and pots with the yellow and white towel that hung on the dish rack. Each item was placed in the cabinets in its proper place.

Partially dressed, Bree heard Mama when she sashayed to her bedroom to have gotten dressed. Daddy was already dressed up by the time Mama entered the bedroom. He pushed pass her and made his way downstairs to the car. Bree's luggage and other things they had bought her for college were placed in the car the night before. Daddy pretended to have made adjustments to the suitcases, and moved them to a different place. Eventually, they were placed back in their original spot in the trunk of the car.

After Bree had checked her hair and new outfit in the mirror, she peered out the window into the distance and briefly wondered what was ahead, what would be left behind, and what life at the house would be like after she had left.

"Are you ready? We better get down to the car, before he starts," Mama said in an unusually pleasant voice. They moved to the bottom of the stairs, as Bree tagged behind Mama with a smile because of

163

the pleasantness in the air.

Daddy paced around the car. Bree pondered what was truly on his mind. He was dressed up in one of his better Sunday-go-to-meeting suits and had toned down the color to a more sophisticated and classy color of navy blue, pinstriped, with a matched solid navy-blue vest. His suits were kept spotless by Mama, or she would have paid the price. He was known to have carried on swearing like three gallons of crazy in a two-gallon bucket. Bree was ecstatic when she saw he had decided to not have worn one of his usually bright and bold colored leisure suits. Dreadfully bright suits that had not complimented his dark skin tone. He just looked like a hot mess.

Mama looked extremely pretty in her floral printed empire waist dress. Her round and caramel brown face seemed to sit in the middle of a bed of pink, yellow, red, and white roses. The fake pearl earrings that matched made her look like the pictures of Jackie Kennedy in the history books and on TV. Skin toned stockings, tan shoes with heels, and a tan shoulder strapped purse made Mama's outfit to have appeared as if it came straight out of a magazine. A gift from Aunt Mamie.

"Are you ready? "Bree was asked again while she stood in the kitchen by Mama.

"Yes ma'am, I'm nervous, though," she answered with mixed excitement that seemed to have traveled in all directions.

At that moment, Mama did something she had never done before. She turned and looked into Bree's eyes. With an unexpected grab, she embraced Bree with one of Grandma Lilly's bear hugs.

"You are going to be fine, Bree." Mama nodded.

They piled into the car, and Bree sat in her normal spot behind Mama. After the hug, she felt a slight connection. Junior sat on the swing she had used so many years as her haven. Daddy backed the car into the driveway, and she caught a glimps of Junior's face. He shot his middle finger towards the car. The picture of Junior on the tire swing stayed with her, and she wondered why was he so angry?

On August 8th of 1976 on a beautiful, bright sunny autumn Sunday afternoon, Bree officially flew the barren coop she knew. This was the day she became officially indoctrinated into a new type of family. She sat in the backseat of the Sedan Coup de Ville Cadillac Daddy had bought and paid cash for a month before. Her oomph was high as a kite as she had prepared her mind for the journey of the day ahead.

"Here I come, here I come South Carolina State," was the chanted message she had sent to the universe, and the universe chanted back, "The world is your oyster. Go make a pearl, girl."

Once the car reached the turn to Highway 301, her mind shifted away from her brother and the house.

165

She was captivated by the tranquility of the ride, and the vast landscapes that stood between them and the car. This was the first time she had been this far away from the house. The new car smell permeated as they drove the open highway. The interstate was between rows and rows of crops planted with the same, exact precision. Oversized southern colonial style homes made spotted appearances from behind perfectly aligned Magnolia and Pecan trees. Such breathtaking scenes of real-life southernism epitomized what she had seen in her history books, and on movies on TV. The mood of the car seemed to have an unnatural calmness, especially after they had just come off such a whirl wind ride with Junior.

"We still have a while to go, maybe about another twenty-five to thirty miles," Daddy announced from the front seat after he had driven for roughly fifteen minutes. He cautiously drove the speed limit as he reached the outskirts of a small town named Bamberg. Bree saw an entrance sign ahead, and read the engraved words out loud, "Bamberg, South Carolina. Chartered 1855."

The small town was filled with settlements of history from the Depression Era. Quaint little country grocery stores and windows filled with dressed up mannequins. Daddy waited on the only red light to have changed to green, and the car moved to the outter skirts of the small town.

She leaned back and relished the serenity of the ride. Her mind drifted into a place of the unconventional thoughts she had experienced when her life went into a dark place. Up until this moment, her life had proven to have been extremely difficult and problematic. Although, she had experienced some highs in her senior year because of her love of painting and writing. She smiled when she thought of the senior's award's program, where she had read the poem she had entered in the school's writing contest that had won her first place. Such pride as she stood before her senior class and all her teachers, but most importantly, Mrs. Buxton. Mrs. Buxton stood and applauded when she had ended her poem. The entire class stood, and Cheryl gave her best friend a wink. Sammy's loud whistles were heard all over the gym.

Bree's mind settled into a more pleasant and peaceful place, still excited about what was up the road ahead. She dozed into a coma-like state as her eyes closed gradually. The dream she had in the Déjà vu green pastures with the beautiful and majestic horse, resurfaced. But this time, the season had changed to fall. Golden tones of autumn colored leaves drifted one by one from it's peaceful place in the tree tops. Each glided by the wind to it's new home below where it would in return fertilize the earth's floor with love. Faded bird chirps were heard vaguely in the distance. The smell of Mother Earth in the dream, signified it was her season in life to have sown new seeds. Grains that had been harvested and sifted; and from the grains that remain a new season of growth was generated.

The car hit a bump.

"Must have been something in the road. Probably a possum or something else dead," Daddy explained out loud to himself.

Bree woke up washed down in sweat. She reached and mashed the button that lowered the window.

"Why are you putting that window down?" Daddy asked with an irritated and scratchy throat.

"It's hot, that's why. Maybe if you cut some air on, it wouldn't be so hot sitting in all this hot sun," Mama snapped back.

Her nap was officially over once they started. She thought for sure the madness between them would have lasted the remainder of the trip. Bree hit the button on the door as the window moved back into its original position. As soon as the car's window was back in its regular position, the conversation ended.

"Well, that's a first, "Bree mumbled with shock.

"We are almost there, we made good time," Daddy stated proudly, with a smidge of arrogance. They had reached the welcome sign at the entrance of the city.

"Welcome to Orangeburg, South Carolina, home of Edisto Memorial Gardens." Bree once again read the sign out loud, but this time she smiled. Bree saw Mama's eyes as she caught the sight and smell of roses that lined the Memorial Garden. They were engulfed in awe with all the different colors of roses. She rolled the back window of the car down enough to have smelled all the wonderful rosy scents. Mama turned at an angle and looked out Daddy's side of the car. In that moment Mama was touched to have seen the pure innocence for the first time in Bree's face and body language. At that minute, the painful memory of the circumstances of Bree's birth were erased.

Bree lowered the window enough to have stuck her right hand and head into the fresh and bold air. The breeze tantalized her from head to toe. She moved her hand back into the car and poked her tongue outside the car. She drank in the succulent milk of nature as it enticed and filled her body. Bree fondled the sweetness of Mother Earth in her mouth.

"Put that window up, girl. That's too much wind and noise behind my head," Daddy shouted with his head slightly turned in her direction.

"Yes sir," she said in a low voice but loud enough for Daddy to have heard. She sat back in the middle of the seat and brushed her now wild hair back down with both hands.

"Now, when you get there, there at school, you need to be careful. You are going to be around people you don't know. You got to be as careful as you can. People are crazier now than they have ever been. They are doing all kinds of unthinkable things to people, killing, and all kinds of foolishness. Don't be in any place other than where you are supposed to be, especially at night. This is your first time away from the house. You have never been any place before now. So do your work and stay where you are supposed to be." Daddy rambled.

"While this whole school thing is good, don't go counting your chickens before they have been hatched. We don't know if this is going to work yet. You struggled with some of your school. I remember your teachers calling the house a lot of times back in the day. I lost count of how many times you and that boy had that phone hot at the same time. Just try to do your best, and the rest will work out. Your Mama and maybe that old looney brother of yours will come and get you from time to time on the weekends. Just do good, you hear me? And don't go taking no wooden nickels from nobody; ha, ha, hew, hew."

He's finally done! She smiled and rolled her eyes to the top of her head before she could have caught herself. Mama rolled her eyes, too, and focused her attention even harder out the side window. The clothesline conversation was hung out to dry because they were almost at the entrance of the campus.

"Yes, sir, I will," she said as she caught Daddy's eyes in the rear-view mirror. I'll be so happy when I'm away from this old man, and all his old stupid sayings. The journey ahead was as crystal clear as the stars that hung in the sky on a moonlit night. She peeled her eyes away from Daddy's when she realized the destination of the day was within view.

"We're here, yawl sit up straight," he barked as they entered the front entrance of the campus. They complied without any hesitation. Bree's eyes danced with ecstasy as they drove beneath the arch at the entrance.

ZOOM ZOOM

"Welcome to South Carolina State College, home of the mighty Bulldogs, Orangeburg, South Carolina." Bree had read the words out loud with suppressed excitement. The campus's entrance was an immaculate picture of pedicured and manicured lawns that were a sight to have witnessed. The school's name was embedded into and surrounded by the thickness of vintage plants, Ivy and Sword Ferns. Such perfection was placed into arrays of flowers with more colors than any human could have counted.

Once again, the entire car was in complete silence. The family was captivated by their views of the campus.

"Wow, oo, look at those flowers," Mama gawked at the rarest flower arrangements she had ever seen.

The campus was packed, and traffic was stop and go all the way to the dormitory. So many buildings with so many names. Named for those whose lives had been claimed. Dr. Martin Luther King, Truth Hall named in honor of Ms. Sojourner Truth, Bethune Hall, and the list went on and on. Bree could not have contained her childlike behavior or stayed still in the seat even if Daddy had hogged tied her with a rope. Quiet as a church mouse, she unclicked her seatbelt, and gently moved to the seat behind Daddy to have gotten a different view. Neither of her parents

173

noticed because they too were in wonderment. Each building along the way drew her in.

"Is this where you are going to be staying?" Daddy asked out loud with an extra country drawl on the end.

"Yes sir, Miller Hall, the one right there," she pointed.

"Yeah, the one over here on this side," Mama repeated. A mid-sized black van backed out and freed up a place for Daddy to have parked closer to the entrance of the three-story building. Miller Hall was an attractively embellished older building designed with old southern charm, reflective of the slave owners' homes she had seen in her history books. She thought that was bizarre since this was a historically black college. Families buzzed back and forth from their cars to the dorm and unloaded luggage, mini-refrigerators, grocery bags filled to the brim with goodies for the next week or two, hot plates, and pots to heat up late-night meals once the dining hall had closed. She eyeballed families engrossed in conversations as they entered and exited her new home away from home.

"Mommy, did you see all the stuff my new roommate had on her bed," a giggly and chatty plump brown skin girl chatted away with her mother as Bree listened in.

"Yes, baby, she is probably going to be a bit messy to live with," the proud mother smiled and wrapped her arm around her daughter's shoulders. Bree with her parents walked like soldiers in a war. One behind the other in straight unison, no signs of affection, no conversations, just stiff strides to the door.

The atmosphere shifted after the door of the dormitory of Miller Hall was opened.

"Wow, this is something else," Bree said, and her spirit connected to the energy of the room. The moment was so surreal. None of her dreams or thoughts, or even what her Cousin Matthew had told her, prepared her for that moment. The dormitory whirled and buzzed with excitement.

"Can you move please, get out the way? This stuff is heavy as heck," an older gentleman said to Bree and pushed his way past her and the others with a mini-refrigerator.

"Move out the way, dag you ain't the only one that needs to get in the building." An overweight girl that looked like a bulldozer, bulldozed her way through the crowd of impatient freshmen students and their families. Those that heard the rudeness, moved over and let the impolite family through.

"Wait, let me get my room key first," Bree said politely to Daddy.

A voice from a girl with long silky black hair moved in front of her.

"Are you in line? We were here earlier, but I forgot to get my room key. My name is Anna, what's yours?

"I'm Bree, Bree Breeze. We just got here, but you can go ahead," Bree said with a friendly and warm smile.

"Nice to meet you, Bree. I hope to see you around campus," Anna said in a very gentle but excited voice with a million-dollar smile.

Bree and her parents stood still as if they were stuck in mud, and watched the parade of activities that moved in front of them. The entrance of the dormitory had been converted into a mass exhibition of what was offered at South Carolina State College. The school's colors of garnett and blue accented every crease and fold that lined the check-in tables that sat unfolded. An African mask adorned the table on each end and a Calathea plant stood out in the middle of the table. Each item on the tables caught its share of bright sunlight from the picture windows on each side of the building.

"Move child, go ahead up to the table and get what you need," Daddy said as he nudged her closer to the table. This snapped her out of her daze, and she cozied up to the table.

"Welcome to South Carolina State College, my name is Millicent, and your name is?" A very charming and attractive second-year student said from behind the table. Her skin and hair glistened and glowed from the stream of sunlight that shined just above her head.

She wore a South Carolina State College t-shirt and light khaki pants. Her complete outfit showed she had selected her attire with great thought. Because she had matched the outfit with a scarf, earrings, necklace, and a bracelet.

"Hi, my name is Bree, Bree, uh, um, Bree Breeze," Bree hesitated and mumbled.

"Okay, Ms. Bree Breeze, it looks like you are in room number 210 on the second floor. Here is your room key, and your folder with your schedule for orientation on Monday. Take the stairs on the right because the other side is for exiting. Have a wonderful freshman year, Ms. Bree," Millicent said with a southern air of elegance.

Bree's eyes were captivated by so many different types of faces. Young souls that searched for their place in the universe at the end of their four year stay at the College.

"Go ahead up the steps so that we can get out the way." Daddy barked at them. She jumped to attention at the sound of Daddy's voice. The jolt of her jump caused her to not have noticed the first step at the bottom of the stairs. She tripped on the step, and the fall became a domino effect as she reached for the rail but grabbed the back of the jacket of the lady in front of her. The entire bottom level of Miller Hall heard, saw, and felt the mortification of all the casualties of the fall. Those around them extended

177

their hands to have helped each of them to their feet.

Lord, the vision of the sight of the fall on the stairs played over and over in her head as if someone had hit the rewind button. They reached the second-floor and looked for room 210. Although the door of room 210 was already slightly opened, she knocked hesitantly, and they entered the room quietly, one behind the other. The room contained three beds, and two were already occupied by her two roommates. Each of them busied themselves with the task of unpacking packed boxes and luggage.

"Hi, you must be Bree," Ashlee said with a catchy smile and an unpredicted laugh that followed. "I'm Ashlee. Ashlee Waters.

Ashlee was very slender and extremely tall for a girl. You must play basketball, Bree surmised in her mind. Ashlee walked from her area of the room and moved closer to Bree and her family as they clung near the door.

"Yes, my name is Bree, and these are my parents," Bree spoke and lowered her head as visions of the earlier incident danced in her mind to the sounds of a not so funky beat. Ashlee was comfortably dressed in a pretty pink blouse and vest that matched her brown plaid knee-length skirt. Her skin tone matched the shade of brown in the vest and pants, which was what made her outfit so unique.

"I'm from a small town called Rock Hill, about an hour and a half away. My dad and mom, and of course, my little brother tagged along, dropped me off three hours ago when the dorm first opened. My older brother Peyton graduated from here six years ago, and he plays for the NFL," Ashlee divulged her family's history without taking a breath. Bree kept quiet and chose not to share any of her family's chronicles.

"Great to meet you," Daddy chimed in from the entrance of the door, not sure if he should have entered.

"You too, sir," Ashlee returned a gesture of politeness with a smile. Although her area of the room looked as if an explosion had occurred. Her warmth drew Bree in like a mild summer's breeze on the beach.

Bree and Mama's eyes met at the same time and locked on Caroline as she began her introduction.

"Hi, I'm Caroline, Caroline Charleston, but my friends call me Carly." She forced the uncomfortable introduction that followed with an uneasy smile. Bree sensed Caroline carried more baggage than what surrounded her area of the room. She was dressed in a very churchy dark brown outfit with stockings and heels like Mama's. Not the appealing shade of brown Ashlee wore. More like that of a grandma on a badly dressed day.

Carly was not as vocal and expressive about her family. She went back to the color-coded stacks she had created on her bed, and then placed them strategically on the shelves of her closet.

Bree walked over to her bed and placed the over-packed suitcase Daddy had lugged from the car. She carried her art portfolio and sat it on her bed. A feeling of disillusionment consumed her as she made quick observations of her new little quaint quarters. Not at all what she had envisioned when she thumbed through the welcome package she had received earlier in the summer. She immediately noticed how cramped the spaces were, with a total lack of privacy between the three of them.

"Where's the bathroom," Bree turned and asked Ashlee with a probing expression.

"It's down the hall, sort of like in the middle of the floor." Ashlee explained. "You know, everyone on this floor shares the same showers and other parts of the bathroom," She finished with a laugh.

"What in the world? Everyone shares the same one?" Bree asked as she looked at Ashlee, totally perplexed and concerned. "How does that work, I mean?"

"Well, it is pretty much first come first served, you wait your turn until someone is done," Ashlee continued, outlining the procedures of bathroom etiquette for dormitory life.

For the next hour, Bree, Mama and Daddy maneuvered up and down the stairs as they brought items from the car to the room. The stairs were a cluttered mess, and most of the time was spent in lines similar to the traffic when they drove on the campus. Many of the overzealous men tried to have carried more than they should have, and often time dropped items in the path of others.

The final trip was completed when she saw Daddy's sweaty and tired face.

"Well, girl that's all your stuff; you should be good for two weeks. That's when your Mama or that boy will be back to get you, and you can come to the house and get the rest of what you need," His voice was as dry as the dirt outside while he looked at Mama.

"Can we go get something to eat before you all leave? "Bree asked.

"Now, I told you before we left the house this morning, I needed to get back before dark," Daddy made his reminder.

This was how he had moved the focus back to himself and his internal needs which were solidified back at the ranch.

"Yes, sir, I understand. I'll just get something from my room, or the dining hall later," she said, and masked her deep let down.

"All right, we are going to head back, be good like I said, and do your best. Call the house if you need something before, we come back," he stated. And without further hesitation, turned and walked towards the car.

She heard Mama mumble very low, "Bye, Bree." No hugs or "I love you" that Bree had heard other families shared when they had departed.

The air outside this time seemed a lot clearer, and the load of the day had gotten lighter after her parents drove away in the big pink Cadillac. The crisp and fresh August air on the campus emptied Bree's mind of all the clutter she had experienced over the past several hours. She forgot about her hunger, and decided to have explored the campus instead. The late and lavish Sunday afternoon's sun was exhilarating and motivated her steps as she strolled around the larger than life campus. The velvety smooth touch and aromatic smell of the immaculate flower beds that sat in front of Manning Hall in a circular shape whispered to Bree through Mother Earth's gentle voice.

She came across a flimsy little metal sign that hung between two protected chains, faded and worn with time that read, "Do not touch." Bree read the words, but chose to have ignored them. Without a thought or care, she cleared the chains and heeded her own call.

In the very center stood the white roses, symbolic of purity associated with her soul. She grinned inwardly. There were also yellow, pink, and orange roses which represented the friendship, gratitude, and fascinations from her past. She gently touched and stroked one of the many red roses with her fingertips as she desired passion and love, and not just from above.

"Is that the girl that fell on the stairs?" A chubby, looks-challenged girl asked her companion as they both pointed and giggled at Bree.

"Yes, that was so funny," said the other girl through her laughter, looking just as evil-as her companion.

Bree looked in the opposite direction and removed herself from her peaceful place in the bosom of the Garden of Eden.

"Whatever, you two heifers," Bree said as she rolled her eyes at the two.

The fiery energy Bree had felt earlier fizzled out, and she found herself very tired. She walked back to the dorm, and maneuvered her way up the stairs to her room. Both of her roommates were gone, and she welcomed the emptiness of the room. She laid across her bed, and immediately fell asleep.

Not certain of what time of day it was, Bree heard music from outside her window. Carly and Ashlee walked in as Bree moved to the edge of her bed.

"Look, Bree and Carly, it's a big party in the street, look come here, you two," Ashlee shouted as she moved from the door to the window. Ashlee's bed was near the window; therefore, she had prime access to the shenanigans outside. Bree jumped from the bed and ran to the windows at the front of the dormitory. They both kneeled on Ashlee's bed and felt the energy of the music and people that danced in the street. Carly sat at her desk with her back turned. Bree and Ashlee looked at each other and shrugged their shoulders.

A large group of students had congregated in front of the Student Union Center across from the entrance of the dormitory.

"Wow, our first party, "Ashlee said with an eagerness that Bree felt as well.

"Come on, Ashlee, let's go outside in the street," Bree shouted as she and Ashlee both jumped from the bed. This was the first time Bree had been to a party since her outing after graduation night. The dj pumped the soulful beats of the seventies. When their feet hit the pavement they shook their groove things to Parliament Funkadelic's, "Flashlight." The speakers pumped out sounds that seemed to have reached to the sky.

Flash Light Now,

I lay me down to sleep, ooh,

I just can't find a beat

Flashlight Flashlight Flashlight Flashlight.

Bree and Ashlee sung along with the song and to each other. The two new friends were having the time of their lives. Then the music grind to the slower beat of Lionel Richie and the Commodore's, Zoom.

I may be just a foolish dreamer,

But I don't care.

Cause I know my happiness is waiting,

Out there somewhere.

Bree's mind drifted back to earlier in the day when she had found peace and serenity in the bosom of the garden. But then, just like earlier, she was pulled from her trance by a voice. The voice this time came with a question from the opposite sex.

"Hi, my name is Kenneth, but my friends call me Ken. Would you like to dance?" She looked at Ashlee, and Ashlee looked back. "Not you, the other one in the yellow," Kenneth pointed at Bree. She hesitated before she had answered. A flashback of her prom night when she and Sammy danced the night away came to mind. Bree smiled when she thought of all the silly dances he had done, and she felt the warmth of a smile come across her lips. She knew that if Daddy had known, he would have had a fit.

"You going to end up with a child on your hip, messing around with them old nappy head boys."

185

"Do you want to dance?" The voice asked again, this time with more authority. She zoned her mind back into the moment, and murmured dubiously, "Yeah, I guess?" Just as he reached and placed his arm around her waist, the words of the song seemed to have gotten louder.

Well, I've shared so many pains

And I played so many games

Ah, but everyone finds the right way

Somehow, some way, someday

Woah, zoom, I'd like to fly far away from here

Where my mind can see fresh and clear and I'll...

The song ended. Bree blew a big sigh of relief.

"Whew!" She turned, and attempted to walk back over to where Ashlee stood alone.

"I didn't get your name, Ms. Lady. Where are you going so fast?" Uncertain of what to say, Bree pretended to not have heard the stranger. Ken, though, was persistent and continued to chase after her.

"Hello, where are you going so fast?"

She gave in, and stopped in her tracks.

"I'm Bree."

"Where are you from? "Ken threw questions at her like the left-handed pitcher "Louisiana Lighting" of the New York Yankees.

"I'm from Charlotte, North Carolina. I got a four-year academic scholarship in music. Charlotte is a nice city, not too far from Carowinds. I live with my Mother and two younger sisters, Mable and Inez. Bree tuned Kenneth out and cut the conversation off.

The dj played "Rapper's Delight" by the Sugar Hill Gang.

Bree's head started to move, and bobbed up and down to the beat. She continued to have ignored him.

He is kind of cute, but way too weird, she thought. He talked way, way too much, and she was never afforded an opportunity to have said anything but her name. He just blathered on and on with what turned to a bunch of mumbo jumbo with no end.

God, he is about as confused as a fart in a fan factory. I got to get away from this fool Bree thought. Then she made her way into the crowd. Is this what they are all like? Is this what I thought I'd missed out on? Bree questioned the stars that lit the sky.

"No more separating. Agree?" Ashlee said, and she and Bree made a promise.

"Let's go see the different things under the tents," Bree said in Ashlee's direction.

"Yeah, we can still hear the music, and you can get away from that weirdo," Ashlee added and laughed her unique laugh. They locked arms and skipped down the sidewalk that Bree had traveled earlier that day. Bree was mesmerized by the unique art she saw. She stood and stared until Ashlee pulled her to a table with an assortment of jewelry. They both tried on necklaces and bracelets, and dangled big ear rings from their ears.

"Look Bree this is a bad top," Ashlee grabbed a top that moved back and forth from the wind of the fan that sat underneath the table.

"Wow, I want that!" Bree snatched the top from Ashlee and held it against her body. She reached into her pocket to have seen how much money she had.

"What size is it, Ashlee?

"It's a small." Ashlee told Bree and smiled.

"How much is it?" Ashlee asked the patient lady that stood on the opposite side of the table.

"For that one I will let you have it for $15.00. Normally it sells for $25.00.

"I'll take it." Bree beamed and paid.

"Not bad, my friend." Ashlee winked at Bree.

The big welcomed party ended, and the two walked the short distance very slowly back to their dormitory.

"Is that who I think it is? Please tell me my eyes are playing tricks on me?" Bree looked at Ashlee dismayed.

"Yep, that's your new nutty dance friend," Ashlee teased Bree with a hint of concern. Kenneth sat on the stoop of the dorm and waited for his one dance partner's return.

"Hey, you left and didn't say anything. Just wanted to make sure you were okay," Kenneth said to Bree.

Bree looked to Ashlee for an answer.

"What do you want?" Bree questioned Kenneth with great uneasiness.

"Good night," Ashlee snapped at Kenneth. Then they ran up the stairs to the second floor.

"Wow!" the two said simultaneously out of breath. They reminisced and laughed out loud about their first campus outing, Bree laid flat on her back and searched for answers, about Kenneth. The why's and why nots of it all.

"Well, he is kinda cute." Bree reasoned this was the only positive thing she could have found in her mind.

But she somehow felt perhaps everything that glittered certainly was not gold, especially when it came to him.

She looked at the back of Carly's head while she sat

at her corner desk, and read in silence scriptures from her worn black Bible.

The porch light was on, but Lord have mercy nobody was home, more crazy than cute. Bree sneered.

RISE AND SHINE

Carly's alarm clock blasted the three awake. One by one, they popped straight up in their beds like chipmunks that had burrowed beneath the ground.

"Good morning, yawl. How did everybody sleep? What are we supposed to do today?" Ashlee asked as she stretched her arms above her head. She reached for the folder she had received when she arrived, but it fell to the floor.

"At nine, we need to be at the MLK Building for our new student orientation," Carly spoke for the first time since her painstaking introduction.

"Oh, that's the building at the entrance with all the nice plants and flowers," Bree interjected as she yawned.

"Guess we better go try out this bathroom thing and take a shower," Ashlee said with great hesitation.

"Oh yeah, I forgot all about that," Bree said to her new-found friend.

"Here, I have an extra tray. Put everything you will need for the shower in this and hang it over the shower head. Do you have a shower cap for all that thick hair?" Ashlee ensured her friend was taken care of prior to their departure. Carly wrapped herself tightly in her fluffy pink floor-length bathrobe and left the room. Bree and Ashlee were still in mid-conversation. They looked at each other, and shrugged again, dismayed by Carly's abrupt rudeness.

After their morning's bathroom tasks were taken care of, Bree and Ashlee returned to the room. Carly was fully dressed and ready to go. She had changed from the dark brown churchy outfit she wore when she had arrived to a dark brown tent-shaped dress.

"Not as bad as I thought it would have been," Bree said to Ashlee. She dressed in one of the new outfits Cousin Matthew had sent her from California. She loved the bright and bold colors and the yellow background. Ashlee decided on golden plaid pants with tan accents and a white blouse.

Once again, Kenneth sat on the stoop.

"Good morning, Ms. Bree and ladies," Kenneth said as he quickly jumped to his feet. Carly was behind Bree and Ashlee and looked on with her ears set on high volume. Bree jumped before she had caught herself.

"What are you doing here?" Ashlee asked.

Bree gathered her composure and moved to the bottom step.

"What do you want?" She snapped at Kenneth with bitter annoyance.

"Come on, Bree, leave that whacko alone, he's c-r-a-z-y," Ashlee said as loudly as she could have with her eyes on Kenneth. He completely ignored Ashlee, and continued.

"Hello Bree. Nice seeing you, can I talk to you?" Kenneth tried to get Bree's attention away from Ashlee.

"Go away, nutsy! Leave her alone, you psycho!" Ashlee screamed at Kenneth.

Others that had left their buildings for the new student orientation stopped and stared.

"Okay, lean, mean giraffe," Kenneth said to Ashlee.

Laughter erupted

Kenneth finally got the message and hung back as a crowd headed to the auditorium. Bree found herself crushed yet again with whispers of her incident with the campus weirdo.

Bree's second day of new beginnings, and she had two strikes in the first inning. The three entered the packed auditorium, and Bree felt a rush of high energy.

"Hey, over there. I see three seats over there," Carly said as she pointed to the third row near the stage.

"Too close. It'll be hard to see from there," Ashlee ignored Carly and picked out three seats in the center of the auditorium higher up.

193

"Yeah, I like those better," Bree said and agreed with her friend. Carly rolled her eyes but followed them to the center row seats. Ashlee plopped down in the center seat, and Bree and Carly found their spots on each side. Bree noticed Kenneth sat two rows down when he waved to her. She quickly looked at her folder and ignored him. Ashlee saw him as he waved and returned the wave with four of her fingers in the down position.

"Good morning and welcome to South Carolina State College, home of the mighty Bulldogs and the Marching 101 Band! My name is Janice Jacobsen, and I am a sophomore. My major is Theater Arts with a minor in Visual Arts. It is both an honor and a privilege to stand before you today and welcome you to this amazing school and your home away from home. If you are anything like I was when I started, you are sitting there feeling a million different emotions and asking yourself a million different questions. Like, did I make the right choice? Was this worth the sacrifices I have made to get here? Let's hope you are not the admissions mistake. Chuckle Let me tell each of you that you are here because you deserve to be. Each of you bring something new and exciting to our school. To the future graduating class of 1980, welcome to South Carolina State College," said the girl that greeted Bree at the table. She was now at the center of the stellar stage, and still carried the same exuberant energy and affectionate smile.

Bree's eyes caught the strangeness of Kenneth's reaction to the Theater Arts student. She tapped

Ashlee, and pointed in his direction. He sat at the edge of his seat with his tongue partially out of his mouth.

"I told you he was weird, look at him," Ashlee said in an attempted whisper.

"Shh, be quiet," Carly said as she tapped Ashlee's elbow. Others around them chanted the same shhs.

Janice finished her speech to the future class of 1980.

"Class of 1980, you have a charge to lead. Make your four years have a purpose. Not just for your life, but for the lives of others and the world. Thank you."

The three roommates listened to speaker after speaker and the morning drug into what had now become afternoon. It was time for lunch. The school's president, Dr. Marrow, walked to the podium.

"Students, we will take an hour's break for you to enjoy lunch in the Washington Dining Hall, right across the garden court. Our cooking staff has prepared a delicious meal, and we are very assured you will enjoy the variety. Please bow your heads as I bless the food."

 Carly whispered soft "amens" and "praise Gods" after each break in the long-winded prayer. "Amen!" the entire auditorium shouted when Dr. Marrow's prayer finally ended.

"Whew, he took long enough. He must have been an old Baptist preacher in another life," Bree said and chuckled. Ashlee laughed out loud, but Carly rolled her eyes as she placed a greater distance between her and her roommates.

They lingered behind Carly and laughed and talked about how boring the morning had been.

"Hi, Ms. Bree." Bree knew the voice instantly. But she pretended to not have heard it, Ashlee did. Carly slowed her pace. This had become the most excitement she had since her arrival because she had stayed in and unpacked while the others danced the night away under the stars. She had read her required hour of Bible scriptures instead. Her roommates were proving to be the best entertainment on the campus.

"Just keep walking and ignore him," Ashlee commanded her friend.

The overpowering smell of the various foods Dr. Marrow described hit them in the face without any warning. They had all missed breakfast, so the buffet style lunch was truly a festive feast for the eyes and stomach to behold. The same dj from the night before had moved his turned table, microphone, and speakers to the far end of the dining hall by the windows. Windows so clear and clean it made it seemed as if no glass existed. He pumped his musical talents through the dining hall, and the stagnated mood of the morning had turned to an ambiance of uninhibited energy.

"He must have been in the church choir," Bree said to Ashlee about the dj.

"Why?" Ashlee inquired of her friend.

"Cause he ain't nothing but treble." Ashlee's laugh was heard all over the lunchroom. Carly caught herself as she felt a small smile, and she immediately pulled it back.

"That's a good one," a voice from behind said with a laugh.

"Hi, I'm Janice, I remember you from yesterday. Sorry about what happened with you on the stairs." Ashlee and Carly turned in Bree's direction with puzzled looks. Janice assured Bree her concern was real.

"Thank you, Janice. It is nice to meet you. These are my roommates, Ashlee and Carly."

"Hurry up, girl, yawl holding up the line. People got to eat," a heavy country accent interrupted their conversation.

"Hold your horses farmer in the dell, your horse outside ain't going nowhere," Ashlee said to the homely five foot nothing country Bama that stood behind her. He looked even shorter because Ashlee was exceptionally tall for a girl.

"Uh," he murmured and took two steps back.

The newly formed group made their final selections from the enticing smorgasbord. Janice led the group over to an open table for four by a wall of exquisitely carved out windows adorned with delicately placed plants.

"What happened yesterday?" Carly asked after taking a sip of her tart lemonade. Bree looked at Janice before she spoke.

"Well, I wasn't looking at where I was stepping and I missed the bottom step of the stairs. I grabbed the back of this lady's jacket in front of me instead of the rail, and she fell. My Mama was right behind me, and she fell as well. We all fell. We all fell thanks to me. Guess the stairs must have been up to something, yawl," Bree chuckled, and the others joined in.

After a great lunch, the bunch casually walked back to the auditorium for the afternoon session of the orientation. Bree now laughed about the memory on the stairs. The laughter healed her hurt and removed those feelings that felt like she had been trampled in the dirt.

She taught herself today, how to have laughed at herself.

Bree saw Kenneth standing by the first set of double doors to the entrance of the MLK Building. He looked like he had just escaped from a mental institution. She immediately herded the lunch bunch to the second set of doors. Janice said her goodbyes and headed back to the stage. Bree, Ashlee, and Carly searched and found three seats together near the back of the auditorium this time.

"Welcome back, students of the class of 1980. My name is Jessie Hammonds, and I am one of the drum majors for the Marching 101 Band. I am a junior, majoring in Music Education," Jessie informed his captivated audience. Two of the other drum majors stood in formation to each side of him with their hands placed in identical places on their batons. Jessie blew his whistle three times, and each snapped to attention. The whistle was blown three more times, and from the aisles the band filled the auditorium generating raw excitement. Ashlee leapt to her feet, and signaled Bree to join her when the band belted out Earth Wind and Fires' "Sing a Song." The girls sounded like a church choir as they sang the words:

When you feel down and out Sing a song,
It'll make your day yeah yeah
Here's a time to shout
Sing a song, it'll make a way
Sometimes it's hard to care
Sing a song, it'll make your day
A smile so hard to bear
Sing a song, it'll make a way

Sing a song
Sing a song
Sing a song

199

"Wow, what a difference from that boring old stuff this morning," Ashlee yelled in Bree's direction above Carly's head. Carly remained seated.

"Yeah, Ash, I like this," Bree said as she snapped her fingers and moved to the loud beat. The high energy of the band exited the auditorium, and without missing a beat, the sounds of clappers and stompers hit the stage. "Introducing, Introducing Ahh, AHH Omega," each line of stompers made circles in and out on the stage and came to an abrupt stop at the edge. The stage was covered with members that represented all the sleek and stylish sisterhood of Greek sororities and the rugged toughness of the Greek brotherhood fraternities.

The program ended with information distributed about the first football game, homecoming in September, the Debutant Cotillion in November on the fifth of nobody cares, pep rallies, parties, and the list went on and on.

Janice concluded the program with a reinforced, "Welcome to South Carolina State College, graduating class of 1980. Have an amazing freshman year." The air cleared from all the animation. Bree and her crew with all the students filed out of the auditorium. They chatted about the band, the steppers, homecoming, and Greek life parties.

"Well, it's two o'clock. What's next, ladies?" Ashlee asked. Bree flipped her folder open, found the time slot, "It says we have to meet with our academic advisors to go over our first semester schedules."

Students maneuvered their bodies from the almost day long activities and prepared their minds to have met with their academic advisors. With her drained brain and her folder tucked neatly under her arm, Bree sat amongst the other art majors that waited to meet with Dr. Nickolas. Once again, she found herself in a nervous place in the midst of jittery strangers. Dr. Nickolas debuted from her neatly tucked away office with the perfect view of the breath-taking flowers. She was the most attractive person Bree had ever seen in her life.

Wow, look at her deep chocolate smooth skin, and hair that looks like the puffy white clouds seen in the far distance. Bree was awe-struck.

Professor Nickolas gathered the small group into the Art Department's lecture hall. She spoke with such elegance and grace as she meticulously explained the department's role and the requirements for them to have worked towards in order to have graduated in four years. .

"There are a few of you I will need to see in my office after you have received your schedule. Your schedule will have a 'see me' attached."

Bree felt a pinched feeling in her stomach. Her mind drifted back to the meeting with Mrs. Buxton, her high school guidance counselor. The meeting when she was told her grade point was just slightly above the requirement for entrance, and her math and science classes were not good. Then names were called, and schedules handed to their rightful owners. Bree already knew when she reached for her schedule a note would have been attached.

The small lecture hall seemed like a big body of uncharted water. She felt like a fish that had been bitten by a shark and now laid wounded in the infested waters after she had gotten the white sheet. The fun of the day was now completely gone because everything had turned real.

"Man, oh man, what a rotten deal." Bree's edgyness kicked into high gear. The uneasiness she felt spilled over while she sat and waited her turn to be called into the serenity of Dr. Nickolas's sanctuary. She twisted and turned and chewed on her bottom lip.

"Ms. Breeze," a student assistant said looking into the crowd of uneasy faces.

"Yes, ma'am," Bree managed to have mustered up the words as she raised her petite body from the chair.

"Good afternoon, Ms. Breeze. How are you doing?"

"Good afternoon, Dr. Nickolas. I am doing good."

"Welcome to South Carolina State College, Ms. Breeze. We are so elated you have decided to attend our school in preparation for your future. Our Art Department is one of the top in the state. I have seen some of the amazing pieces from your portfolio. You are a very gifted and talented artist that will contribute much to the field and the world of art."

"Thank you, ma'am," Bree said as she wondered why she had been summoned into the office.

"Ms. Breeze."

Here we go...

Dr. Nickolas placed the first semester schedule in the center of the desk Bree sat across from. "You seemed to have struggled with some of your classes in high school, and parts of the SAT. Namely, your math scores stand out the most. Ms. Breeze, with that being said, if you look at your schedule, you will notice you have Math 100. Do you see it here at the bottom?"

"Yes, I mean yes ma'am."

"It is a remedial class. The class is for the first semester only to help prepare you for Math 101 in the Spring semester. It's more like a tutoring type of class to help get you on track. You will do well, and move on to your regular math with success. Do you understand?" Dr. Nickolas assurance made her feel somewhat better.

Bree left Dr. Nickolas' office with a slight sense of relief but knew how unprepared she was for this day. Reality stared her straight in the face.

"I have started my journey behind," she realized and sadly told herself.

Bree decided to take the stairs to the bottom floor and not the elevator she had ridden up on with the others. The stairs seemed to be the best choice. She wanted the silence of the stairs to have cleared the sting of the conversation. The last step was a reminder of yesterday's fall.

Today another type of fall.

A slow walk past the flowers she had admired on her arrival. She moved sluggishly away from the murky madness of Professor Nickolas's meeting and headed back to the dorm. The room was empty, and she took this as the perfect opportunity to have taken a nap on her cozy little bed by the door. She wrapped her entire body in the fluffy pink blanket that layered the foot of her bed. Her body swayed and rocked until the tiredness of the day lulled her into a deep sleep.

She was awakened by a door that had been slammed too hard. Jolted by the sound, Bree snapped to an instant attention position. She pulled herself to the edge of the bed still wrapped from head to toe in the blanket. Still alone in what had seemed to be a big empty barn. With her face in her hands, she cried uncontrollably.

THREE STRIKES: PRESS ON

Three days of a rollercoaster ride orientation ended, and Bree had finally unpacked her last piece of luggage. She had settled into the bathroom and bedroom routines of Miller Hall. Quite a bit to have learned in such a short period of time. Ashlee and Bree hung out more and more, and Carly took comfort in her evening Bible reading sessions alone at her desk. Bree shared with Ashlee what she was told at her academic advisement meeting.

"It's okay, Bree. You take a semester of that math, and you'll be back on track, right?"

"I guess so, maybe, I hope," Bree said with apprehension.

"You will be fine. Fine as the hair on a frog's behind! Come on girly, let's go to the Student Center and grab a bite to eat. Then we can go to this party I heard about, "Ashlee convinced Bree to get out of the room and away from the weirdness of Carly.

Ashlee had overheard some of the freshmen as they talked in her academic advisement session about a party one of the sororities was having at their sorority house. It was the last party before their classes started. When she saw Bree was in a funky place, Ashlee knew she had to have rescued her new friend.

"It's one of those sororities we saw on the stage. My brother told me about these kinds of parties," Ashlee said, and grinned. Bree nodded and took long strides to have kept up with Ashlee and her long legs.

The sorority house was packed from the front door to the back door, and from every window to all the walls. Ashlee pushed her way through the crowd and pulled Bree by her right arm to the dance floor.

No, weirdo, Kenneth tonight Bree smiled to herself. The speakers that sat in each corner of the room blasted the O'Jay's "Love Train." Bree could not believe she was in such a horrible place earlier. The song ended, and they pushed through the pack of hot and steamy bodies to the kitchen area of the house. They both grabbed cups of punch from the table. Thirsty with no thought to what was in the cups, they gulped the contents and reached for another.

"Look what the cat drug in," Ashlee blurted out.

"Hello, beautiful. Do you want to dance?" Kenneth stood within inches of Bree's face. He grabbed her hand, and pulled her into his body. Before she could have pulled away, Kenneth slammed his lips into hers and kissed her. Bree's first kiss. She was shocked, and not sure of what feeling consumed her body. Was it the joy from the cup, or a high from the kiss?

Um, wait a minute, that felt good. She stood stunned.

Ashlee rambled on and on with how gross that was. The kiss must have casted a spell because without a word spoken, she followed Kenneth to the dance floor. The DJ played, "Zoom." Her mind snapped to attention as she remembered the song from their first encounter. Déjà vu. Through the fogginess in her mind, she danced with unassured but joyous thoughts. Ashlee looked like an overly protected Mama that had caught her child doing something wrong. She watched her friend dance in Kenneth's' arms. In her anger, Ashlee left the party without her friend. Bree allowed Kenneth to have walked her back to the dorm since she was alone.

Bree laid silently in the dark and felt the strangeness of Ashlee's vibes across the room. She stared at the ceiling as feelings from the kiss lulled her to sleep.

Bree awoke in the morning with a new surge of get-up-and-go. She pulled her schedule from the folder that sat on the desk next to her bed.

"Ugh, math at 9. Rise and shine." Bree blurted the words out loud. She was reminded of the class that would not have counted towards her graduation. Reminded of how she had started out behind. She grabbed her shower kit and headed unhurriedly to the collective bathroom.

"You know that weird boy that always sits on the stoop and waits for that girl down the hall with all that wild hair. Well, I heard he likes boys," one of the girls that stood at the sink said while she brushed her straight hair back into a ponytail.

"Oh, really, they say that tall girl, she's around all the

time likes girls," the other girl at the sink said while she brushed her teeth and gargled with the travel size Listerine. Bree stood stunned by the words in the shower she had overheard between the two.

What are they talking about? She waited for the chatty girls to have left before she stepped from the shower. Confused by what she had heard, she quickly dried her body with the cottony pink towel, and wrapped herself in her white bathrobe. She stepped beyond the shower doors, and the chill in the air snapped her back like a lasso that was used to have captured a baby calf in a rodeo.

Ashlee entered the bathroom and gawked in her direction.

"Good morning," Bree said to Ashlee, uncertain of what else to have said.

"Morning," Ashlee sluggishly said in her direction and headed straight to the shower. Her head still pounded from the cups of punch she had drank at the party.

Bree's heart felt sunken.

"Welcome to Math 100!" Professor Morris said with a smile.

"Yeah, right, Math for dummies," Bree said to herself.

Professor Morris looked like a student herself with a

smile that quickly overpowered the room. Bree tried but failed to have wrapped her mind around the course syllabus as she theatrically explained each part.

What did they mean Ashlee liked girls and Kenneth liked boys? Her mind fell prey to the bathroom conversation and Ashlee's reaction to her in the bathroom as well.

"That's the end of our first class ladies and gentlemen. See you next Tuesday," Professor Morris announced to the sea of thirty-five uninterested students. Bree had not realized she had spent the entire class period engrossed in such deep thoughts of the bathroom gossip. She finished her last class at three.

"I need a nap. It's been a long boring day. Then I'll go to the dining hall." Bree said as she walked back to the dorm.

"Bree, baby, how are you today?" Kenneth asked as he sat in his favorite spot on the stoop. Her mind searched for a response. Before a single word was spoken Ashlee's long strides brought her to the bottom step. All eyes met and locked on Bree. Without any type of response, the mystified look in her eyes said it all.

Bree had become confused and overwhelmed with things she had experienced with her classes, Kenneth, and Ashlee. She knew her Mama wouldn't have an answer. She waited for an opportunity when the phone in the hallway was free, and she called her cousin Matthew. After she had paced from one end of the hall to the next, the hall phone was finally available. Bree sprinted to the phone and grabbed the receiver off the hook.

"Hello Mat," Bree said as she held back tears.

"What's wrong, Bree?"

Bree talked until she was interrupted by a pesty visitor in need of the phone.

"Thanks, Mat, I will talk to you soon," Bree said to her cousin before she had hung up the phone neatly and cautiously in the busy hall. She had decided to have called her cousin when she was unable to have understood the conversation in the bathroom.

The first semester of Bree's freshman year ended, and it was time for the almost three-week Winter break. Needless to say her grades had struggled. She was at her wits end with Ashlee because she had become horrible to her verbally. What her mouth hadn't communicated, her body language showed. The dorm room became as cold as old Professor Fullman's Physical Science class. Bree filled out the form, and requested to have her room assignment changed. After twenty rounds or more of "no's," Daddy paid the extra money. Bree moved to another room of a student that had left before the break. She finally reported Kenneth because he continued to have stalked her after she told him she wanted nothing else to do with him.

"Ms. Breeze, I need to see you after class," Dr. Nickolas instructed Bree on her way into the lecture hall.

"Yes, ma'am," Bree said with the greatest of uncertainty and walked slowly to the front of the room. After class she made her way outside of the lecture hall.

Dr. Nickolas gathered her purse, the papers she had collected, and the leather jacket that matched her plaid skirt and tan turtleneck sweater. Bree and Professor Nickolas carried on small uneventful conversations as they walked to her office. They rode the elevator in silence. Bree felt the knot in her stomach as it had grown tighter. They reached her office.

"Come on in Bree. Have a seat, young lady, please." Dr. Nickolas pointed in the direction of the empty chair next to the window. The view Bree got so much pleasure from. Colors that had so much warmth and calming energy. Blended tones of soothing lilac gray hue and warm pink.

"So, Ms. Bree, how was your first semester?"

"It was okay."

"Just, okay, nothing else to say? I would think you would have more than that to say! Is everything going well for you?"

Bree reluctantly, but finally spoke honestly with her academic advisor. She talked openly for the first time about her classes, the hell in the dorm with her roommates, the mean girls that talked about her, and of course, the nutcase Kenneth. Dr. Nickolas listened intently with compassion to all that she had been through in such a short period of time. Dr. Nickolas did something she had never done with any of her other advisees. She gave Bree a hug and her phone number.

"Bree, this is my personal phone number at home. Call me if you ever need to talk."

Bree's eyes welled up and spilled over with tears. Their conversation lasted well beyond the allotted time she had set aside for their advisement session.

"Thank you, Dr. Nickolas. Thank you for listening to me. I appreciate you more than you will ever know," Bree said with a slight smile.

Dr. Nickolas explained to Bree that during the summer session she would have to retake two of her classes because of failing grades. Her grade point average placed her in jeopardy of academic probation. Dr. Nickolas laid the news about her grades out as gently as possible.

"Bree, I'm going to give you a piece of advice I heard a long time ago from a very wise person, my mother. She would always tell me to don't dwell on the past, and don't daydream about the future, but concentrate on showing up fully in the present moment."

Bree left the office with doubts about her future at college, but her spirit felt less stressed.

How am I going to tell Mama and that old man?

It was Friday afternoon after her last class at three, and Mama waited downstairs in the car. Bree maneuvered the oversized suitcase for her over three weeks stay through a sea of bystanders.

"Hi Mama, how are you doing?" No smiles were exchanged. She was not sure what kind of mood Mama was in.

"I'm good, tired from the drive. Must be a lot of people traveling for the holidays," Mama said with some irritation. Although not as much as usual. Bree slept most of the ride and pretended to have been sleep until they reached the driveway of the house.

No smiling faces were present as she pushed and pulled her suitcase to the bedroom. No sign of Junior or Daddy to be seen. She laid across her bed and pondered how she was going to tell her parents about her grades when Daddy had just paid out extra money for her new dorm assignment. After a brief moment, Bree sluggishly walked down the stairs and back to the kitchen.

"Where's Junior?" The chair scraped across the floor

as it was pulled from the table in the kitchen.

"They are out there in the fields. They'll be here soon for supper." Mama explained with as few details as possible. "How was school? You didn't call here too often. So everything must have been good?"

"It was okay. Some of the classes were hard," she said, as she tried to have soften the blow for what would come later. Their conversation crawled to an uncomfortable halt when Junior and Daddy walked in.

"Well, look what the cat drug in," Junior said and laughed by himself. Bree rolled her eyes. As usual, he was dirty, stinky, and gave out his normal rounds of nastiness.

"Shut- up, smelling like an old dead polecat," Bree said and turned her nose up at him.

"What time did yawl get back?" Daddy questioned Mama but looked in the opposite direction.

"About an hour or so ago, coming back was shorter than going. A lot of traffic today," Mama answered but looked out the kitchen window.

"Is supper ready yet?"

Junior dropped down in his assigned seat, and his dust and funk flung its thickness around the table.

"Go ahead and get washed up," Mama said softly to Junior. It was as if she had tried to have avoided one of his many explosions. Junior heard her, but just sat and leaned back in his chair on the back two legs. He knew how much Mama and Daddy hated this. Mama walked around Junior and placed the bowls of white rice and brown gravy in the center of the table. Junior grabbed two pieces of the golden fried chicken that had already been placed on the table, and placed them on his plate. He started to eat without them.

"Boy, put that piece of chicken down, the food needs to be blessed. Can't you wait for us to sit down? You ain't got any manners, sitting up there disrespecting God," Daddy ranted. Junior just ignored him and continued to chew on the piece of chicken he had already bitten off. Bree watched in silence. It was obvious that in the short period of time she had been gone, things had not changed. She decided tonight would not have been the best time to have talked about school. They finished the delicious meal and went their separate ways.

At breakfast the next morning, before Junior made his presence known, Bree started the conversation with Mama and Daddy about her grades. Silence consumed the house, and they all searched for words to have tried to cut through the thickness. Mama stood with her back turned and looked in her normal direction out the kitchen's window, and made no attempts to have participated.

"Well, gal, what are you planning to do about your grades and school?" Daddy started but was

215

interrupted when Junior entered the room.

"What are ya'll talking about? Don't stop talking, please."

"Boy, go and sit down somewhere. This doesn't have anything to do with you. I swear you'd make a preacher cuss."

"Whatever old man, I bet that one thought you got in your head is really lonely," Junior looked at his father completely disgusted and laughed.

Daddy moved his attention back to the conversation and ignored Junior's words.

"What are you going to do about your grades? All that money I already paid."

Junior sat up in his chair and focused on the conversation.

"Well, Dr. Nickolas said I could retake the classes I failed, and still." Junior interrupted Bree.

"Dummy, you so dumb, that tree out there smarter than you," Junior said to his sister and laughed an evil laugh that covered the entire kitchen.

The joy of the Christmas season disappeared like a popped bubble after the conversation at breakfast. The tension between Bree and Mama and Daddy felt like a rope that had been stretched to its maximum capacity.

For the remainder of her three week stay they avoided conversations about grades and what had happened since she had left a few months earlier. She saw in their faces, shame, and distress towards her. The joy they showed when they had believed for a moment in time in her and school was long gone.

She spent her alone time in her room, and poured her feelings into painting, and cups of joy juice. The comfort she felt after she drank the punch at the sorority party became her go to for times of pain. The highness of that night was re-created over and over with the help of Junior.

He had moved beyond some of his bitterness towards his sister and sympathized with her when he saw how cold Mama and Daddy were. He helped her to have found relief the only way he knew how, in the joy juice he drank down by the pond. At first Bree was reluctant to have indulged, but she eventually gave in.

"I'll drive Bree back to school and help with all that junk she has got to take back. You know, since she got to move from that other place." Bree smiled at her brother because he had helped her get through what should have been a joyous season with the family. He grabbed a piece of the thick-sliced bacon, one of Mama's homemade biscuits, and went out to the tire swing. The swing Bree had not found any time to have swung on during her time at the house.

The second week of January, Bree returned to campus a day early, and moved to her new dorm room. She had not wanted to risk seeing Ashlee or Carly in their once shared room. She thanked her lucky stars because her new room had only one room mate for the new semester.

Bree was confused when she tried so hard to have understood Junior's changed heart. It was very out of character. She knew that on this day she would not have focused her strength on the old Junior, but the newness of the changed one.

The second semester of her first year and Bree made a declaration to the universe that she would work with greater dedication to climb out of the hole she had dug. She reviewed the schedule once again that she had received before the break.

"Well, at least I'm done with that dumb math class," she said to Addison.

Her new roommate, Addison, was a theater major and spent most of her time outside classes auditioning and rehearsing for plays. Addison was very pretty with a bubbly personality and a boat load of corny jokes. She never waited for anyone to have gotten the joke before she burst into the craziest laugh Bree had ever heard. The alone time was what Bree needed after her classes. She took those times to have sipped from the cup she kept neatly tucked away underneath her bed.

Junior made sure her cup never ran dry. He secretly

slipped off the ranch in the middle of the week, or whenever he felt like it and visited her. He brought her what she needed from the house, and re-stocked her supply of the joy juice she had become so fond of.

The semester seemed to have ended in a better place. Although this moment was very short-lived because she knew she would be confined to school for the summer.

"What are your plans for the summer?" Addison questioned Bree one evening as they sat with cups in their hands and toasted to the end of the second semester.

"I have to go to summer school to retake two classes I messed up in. I guess it's better than going back to that God-forsaken house and having to walk around on eggshells all summer. What about you, Addison?" The questions flowed just like the goodness from the bottle that had filled their cups

"Well roomie, I'm going to work in the theater this summer helping with props and where ever I'm needed. The travel group is going to New York on the 12th of June to see a real play. I get to tag along." Addison said and raised her cup up for another round of toasts. This was probably toast number twenty, but who was counting?

"Wow! That sounds exciting, Addison. Can I come with you? I've never been to New York, never really been any place other than here. I have an aunt that lives there, and she is so sweet. I love her so much." The power of the substance in the cup and thoughts of her aunt brought tears to the jovial occasion. "I'm really happy for you, Addison," Bree said.

Though deep down inside, Bree envied her roomie.

The summer of 1977 was a summer filled with the uncomfortable heat on the asphalt streets of the campus. No thrills of parties or the excitement that football and basketball games brought in the fall and spring. The campus reminded her of all the old Western movies she had watched on tv when dust storms moved through and carried thick balls of tumbleweed.

The Summer of 1977 ended, and she was drained. Her grades were only slightly higher than what they were before. Her new-found discovery that Junior had introduced her to, helped her to have completed the summer session with less anxiety. The session on the campus ended with very little downtime before the start of her sophmore year.

She convinced herself to have started her second year with more optimism than when her freshman year and summer school ended. But this was very momentary because her class schedule was riddled with yet another round of the same type of math and science courses. Bree felt frustrated when she viewed her new schedule at the entrance of the registration table. She stood in silence and contemplated the idea that maybe school was not her cup of tea.

Man, here we go again, with another year of this bull it.

She was terrified and felt completely displaced as if she was in a foreign land.

Unclipped wings that had given her a flight to freedom were gone. Burdened down with heaviness, the wind that blew beneath her wings was blocked. She no longer felt the freedom of the birds she admired. Bree no longer wanted to be a part of this institutional confined version of life. She felt a desire to soar to greater heights than where she hovered, stagnated, dying a slow, painful loss of life at low altitude. Feelings of ambiguity announced its presence very loudly in the form of agitation.

But at the end of that year, she had realized with everything in her mind, body, and soul she had not ran this far in the marathon of life just to have given up. Quitting was not an option because defeat was temporary but quitting lasted forever.

Her life too often played out like a video game, just when she felt she had strategically figured out the how, when, where and why, she saw the words, "game over."

She had two options: "Try again" or "End the game."

A NEW DAY BRINGS NEW HOPES

"Good afternoon, Ms. Breeze." A tall, slender man with dark curly hair and skin that matched said from the opposite side of the desk. "I am your new academic advisor, Dr. Graham. Dr. Nickolas was moved to a different department. The reason for our meeting today is to have you declare a major based on your credit hours thus far, okay?"

Confused and not sure at all what he had said.

Bree just said, "Yes sir."

"I feel with your degree in art, you would be better equipped to explore the option of teaching art. This is the most viable option I feel you have. And it would provide you a better opportunity for getting a job after your graduation. With a degree declared in Art Education, your teaching prospects can be explored at an elementary, junior high or high school anywhere in the state. In order to teach, Ms. Breeze, you would need to take, looks like twelve hours of courses in the Education Department where Dr. Nickolas was transferred. She can better help you with which area you would like to pursue. Whether you decide on an elementary or secondary concentration." Dr. Graham continued his conversation and never stopped to have taken a breath. It reminded her of the conversation she had with crazy Kenneth when she had first arrived.

"Take this information with you, and you will need

223

to decide before you register for classes on Thursday."

Bree walked to the end of the campus and found Dr. Nickolas' new office. She was busy with her normal load of advisees because the semester had just begun. She noticed Bree and called her into the warmth of the office.

"Hello, Ms. Bree, how have you been? How were your summer classes?" Dr. Nickolas greeted her with a warm smile and a hug,

"Good afternoon Dr. Nickolas. Summer was very uneventful other than the classes. I did okay with my grades, nothing great. Did you cut your hair? It's pretty like that."

"Thanks, Ms. Bree. You look like you have a lot on your mind, again."

"Yes, ma'am, I'm confused. Dr. Nickolas, I just left Dr. Graham's office, and he said something about declaring a major. I'm not certain what that means. He said I should look at teaching art at a school."

"Yes, he's talking about possibilities for your degree. You are an amazing artist Ms. Bree. But here in the South, very few jobs are available in your field other than teaching. I can talk to some people in the art world and see what other alternatives are available if you are willing to relocate to the North."

"Yes, ma'am, I see. I kind of like the idea of

teaching." She thought back to the art classes she had taken with Mrs. Montfort and how she was one of her favorite teachers. How she had shown her so much kindness although she was white.

"Thank you, Dr. Nickolas, for seeing me without an appointment, and helping me to understand all of this.

"You are very welcome young lady. Have a great day."

Bree left the office feeling better.

At the midway point of her third year, after her major had been declared in Art Education by the

Education Department, Bree's life went into an out of control spiral. She had gotten an override, and took two more classes than was allowed. She wanted to play catch up because she still was not on track to have graduated on time. When she received her grade report, she had three D's in classes she needed at least a C in, and an F in her Elementary Math 110 class.

"What am I going to do? I just can't take this anymore!" Bree shouted to the Universe.

She drug her spiritless body to her room, and sat in silence. After so many cups of what had in the past drowned the pain, she still felt the sharp sting and smelled stench of failure.

On Friday afternoon, after her last class at two, the pink Cadillac sat in the parking lot across from the dorm. Mama was alone for what was goint to be a long ride to the house for the weekend.

"Hi Mama, how are you feeling? Where's Junior?" She questioned Mama as she loaded the small suitcase onto the back seat. She had hoped Junior had picked her up so that the ride would have been less stressful and awkward.

"I'm good today, just tired from the drive. I guess he's out there with your Daddy and the others. He had to work on something that needed to be finished today. Lord knows he wanted to come. Stomping around there all morning like a mad man. Is this all your stuff, are you ready?" Mama asked as she pulled the car slowly and cautiously out of the parking lot and merged into traffic that was leaving the campus for the weekend. They rode in silence and Bree was happy as she pondered how to have explained her position about leaving school.

Late Saturday afternoon, she found an opportunity while the family sat for one of Mama's highly regarded fresh fish fried meals. Still a tradition at the house.

"Um." Bree cleared the pain from her throat. She looked at Daddy at the end of the table.

"You know school is hard, and my grades aren't too good. I'm trying; I'm really doing my best. But these classes are really hard, and well, I just don't feel I'm cut out for this. These classes are really hard now, and my grades are bad. I think it might be time for me to come on back home."

She finished her thoughts, and released the pains of defeat. Daddy showed absolutely no reaction of being surprised.

"If that's what you want to do gal, then just come on back to the house. I told you when you left here to not have put all your eggs in one basket anyway. Your Grandma Mary used to always say you should have a backup plan when the first one doesn't work. The only back up plan I for you, is for you to work out there in them fields with your brother."

The statement shocked and stung like a wasp bite. This was not the response she had anticipated, but none the less typical of Daddy. The implication behind the statement was completely disheartening. Somehow, she knew something was not quite right about what he had blurted out. Based on what she witnessed with Junior's failed attempt to being an educated young black man, she knew what simmered in the pot, stunk like spoiled onions.

They finished their meal, and each went in their separate directions. Dispirited, Bree went off to the swing, dumbfounded. The rest of the weekend was spent in avoidance, again as the family walked lightly around each other as if the house was lined with eggshells.

Sunday's dinner before she and Mama left was more of the same silence. She knew Daddy would never have admitted it, but this had put a strain on his ego. She was the last hope he had to brag about.

The late Sunday afternoon sky was not as clear and blue on the ride back. The space between Bree and Mama in the car seemed to be wider than the windshield that protected them from the brightness of the day. The sunrise had reached for its resting place from the labors of the day. She thought long and hard in the silence of the ride about where she had needed to have channeled her energy. Thoughts about what Dr. Nickolas had told her about her art, and the fact that very few jobs existed in the South for blacks. Maybe it was time she had left her pains and scars of the South, in the South.

The silence and the smooth ride of the car lulled her to sleep. Mama turned the radio to her favorite gospel station and drove to the sounds of James Cleveland's': This Too Will Pass.

I've had heart aches like this before,

And disappointments by the score,

I claim the victory at last,

This too will pass,

I've had heartaches like this before,

And disappointments by the score

I claim the victory at last,

This, too, will pass.

Mama sang along. The peaceful sleep brought a dream that took her into a place of the unknown. Bree had hoped the dream would have shown her what she needed to have known about what laid ahead. Daddy's suggestion hadn't provided any comfort, support, or sensibility for how to have overcome this challenge.

The car stopped at the entrance of her dorm, and Bree waved a heartless goodbye to Mama. She knew Mama had retreated to a place of disappointment because she had resorted back to silence. Her prayers that this was a once in a life time chance for Bree to have made her way to freedom from the ranch, had not been answered.

School had given her more tribulations than triumphs, but Bree knew she had two more years to have made this school thing work, and to have embraced what the universe had stored for her.

On the Monday, after she had gotten back from the house, Bree visited Dr. Nickolas' office. She desperately needed to talk.

"Ms. Bree, when I was a sophomore just like you, my life became riddled with problems and responsibilities beyond my control. My father became ill, and my mother was not able to have taken care of him. She asked that I take a year off and come home to help out. In that year's time, my father passed away, and my mother was all alone. I took a year and a half away from school. The ordeal made me re-think if I had wanted to come back or not. My life was not the same, but I knew I needed to have finished what I had started," Dr. Nickolas eyes filled with tears.

"I'm so sorry, Dr. Nickolas, about your father and your mother's illness." Bree was at a loss for any other words of comfort.

After thirty minutes Bree left Dr. Nickolas' office. She walked slowly, and sat on the bench in the garden. The story touched the core of her heart as she sat in the garden alone, and recalculated her thoughts and gathered her feelings. She sat for an additional thirty minutes before she walked back to her room and laid across the bed. The conversation spoke to her soul that she was not alone.

That no matter what you have gone through, life will go on. That half semester gave a new finished date for December of 1980 and would allow her to have participated in May's graduation ceremony.

THE MORNING AFTER (RETURNING TO THE COOP)

"Neurosis is another word for describing a complicated technique for avoiding misery, but reality is the misery. That is why from earliest times sages have insisted that to see reality; one must die and be reborn." ~ Ernest Becker

Early one chilly spring morning in March of 1981, Bree excitedly prepared and rehearsed her answers for an interview in front of the floor-length mirror in her dorm room in the boarding house on Russell Street she had moved to after her last semester in December.

"Tell us about yourself, and why do you feel we should hire you?" Bree practiced over and over in the mirror.

The college's recruitment center had gotten her an interview with a high school principal for a teaching position in Columbia, South Carolina, which was about thirty minutes away. The job was for an art teaching position.

Bree decided on a perfect navy-blue skirt suit with a white blouse and a single strand of pearls and earrings to have matched. She brushed and teased her thick hair into a ponytail that hung at shoulder length. In the middle of putting on her jacket, she was interrupted by a knock on the door. The voice informed her she had a phone call.

"Bree, you have a phone call, it's your mother," the student at the door shouted and scurried back to her room. Bree knew something was wrong because Mama never called. She always waited for Bree to have made her weekly call. The door slammed behind her as she hurried to the phone. She still had tasks that needed to have been done in order to have not have been late for the interview. When she picked up the phone, Bree felt something was terribly wrong.

"Good Morning Bree, ahem, ahem. How are you doing?"

"Good morning, Mama. I'm okay. I was getting dressed for my interview at the high school. Are you okay?"

"Well, not too good, child. I just left the doctor because I have been feeling poorly lately. He said I'm not doing to good right now, not good at all. I've been going back and forth to the doctor for a while now. They are trying to figure out what's wrong with me, but they don't know yet. I really need you to come back to the house and help me out. You know, help me until I can get better. I don't have anybody here to do things that needs to be done."

De ja vu. Bree's mind drifted back to the conversation she'd had with Dr. Nickolas' from over two years before.

She gathered the belongings that she had accumulated over the past four and a half years and placed them meticulously in the back of Junior's car. Junior had waited uncomplainingly downstairs in front of the twelve-story high rise she had resided in for her last semester at the college. Her feelings ran high as she was pulled in so many different directions. Her heart pumped rapidly and her head spun out of control. And in her soul, she felt completely dampened. But she knew Mama must have needed her, or else she would not have called and asked her to place her life on hold. She was a very prideful woman and as pigheaded as a mule. Bree knew it was serious when she had received the call. They rode in silence the entire trip, other than occasional small talk about gossip.

Her mood shifted to one of sympathy for Mama as she thought beyond their lacking mama-daughter relationship. She thought about how Mama had been through so much in her life. Bree focused on the scenery outside the car's windows, tears blurred the view.

Junior parked in his normal spot off to the side of the driveway under the Magnolia tree by the fish pond. They entered the coldness of the house, and Bree quickly realized there would be no graduation celebration from her family. No welcome home party after the struggles and successes of the past four and a half years.

"What took yawl so long? Must have been a lot of traffic?" Daddy stood in the center of the foyer and belted out questions. The three just looked at each other. Junior turned without a word and walked out the house and towards the pond. It was that time of the day for him because the ride was long. He needed a celebration of his own.

"How's Mama doing?" Bree asked Daddy.

"She's up there in the bed resting, always tired," Daddy said with apathy.

Reality sat in, and once again, the window of opportunity she thought existed was no more than a stained-glass window with beautiful yet imitation images. She found herself back in the place she had left four and a half years earlier.

Bree tried to push her disappointment aside, ignoring all the what-ifs. Like what if she had nailed one of the interviews and had landed a job? And what if she had gotten the job after her second-round interview with a major airline company? What if this had been her ticket to places she had only daydreamed about? She thought of all the places she would have seen, the people she would have met, the exciting stories she would have had to share with friends and family. And what if, for the first time in her life, she could have lived on her own, alone?

The what-ifs were gone and short-lived. Her heart dropped to the bottom of her stomach. She felt her self-esteem plummet even lower as she watched these once in a lifetime chances as they floated away and flickered out into the universe.

"A degree in art ain't worth a fart." Bree mumbled to herself.

She walked to the tire swing, and sat with her back to the house. The house she had no desire to have returned to. The beauty of nature in the backyard was not the breath-taking view it once was. She sat motionless, filled to the brim with baggage that was destined to travel nowhere.

"What are you sitting out here for?" Junior asked his sister as he stood behind her on the old weather-beaten tire.

"No reason, just thinking."

Junior seemed to have been calmer, and that was strange. From the smell that circled around her, she knew he had been drinking. A smell she had become accustomed to as well.

"What are you going to do, since Mama ask you to come back here and take care of her? She has been feeling real bad sometimes. That old man doesn't know how to take care of anybody, especially Mama. Sometimes when it gets really bad, Mrs. Lucille will come and spend the night. Aunt Mamie came a few times when she had been able to have gotten off her job." Junior filled in the gaps for his sister about life at the house since her last visit.

Bree's feelings were all over the place, but she vowed to have made the best of this bitter batch of lemons she had been forced to have squeezed from. These spikey feelings pierced her spirit, like thornes on roses.

She sat alone on the swing with her back still turned to the place she found herself at again. Bree thought of her journey and wondered why she had returned to the coop she flew away from. She thought of a passage by Thomas Wolfe she had read in her literature class:

You can't go back home to your family, back home to your childhood, back home to romantic love, back home to a young man's dreams of glory and of fame, back home to exile, to escape to Europe and some foreign land, back home to lyricism, to singing just for singing's sake, back home to aestheticism, to one's youthful idea of 'the artist' and the all-sufficiency of 'art' and 'beauty' and 'love,' back home to the ivory tower, back home to places in the country, to the cottage in Bermuda, away from all the strife and conflict of the world, back home to the father you have lost and have been looking for, back home to someone who can help you, save you, ease the burden for you, back home to the old forms and systems of things which once seemed everlasting but which are changing all the time—back home to the escapes of Time and Memory.

The house Bree once knew was not the same as it was when she had first left for college. The "Home Sweet Home" sign that hung in the kitchen seemed to be more of a "Home not at all Sweet Home." Mama always kept the house in spic and span shape from top to bottom. The once green plants that surrounded the brightly lit kitchen window had not been watered, or pruned of their dead leaves. They scarcely covered the windows' sill and clung for life onto the dirty faded yellow and white curtains. It was obvious from the looks and smells of the house there must have been days when Mama hadn't the strength to have maintained the house. Everything was dismal and downcast. The sight of it all put Bree in a very despondent state of mind.

She quietly sat in her assigned seat alone in the kitchen. Her mind drifted, and she pondered why she had not noticed Mama's sickness before now. She knew Mama had to deal with Daddy's unscrupulous behaviors and womanizing all her life, but how could she had not seen the sadness in Mama's eyes and her broken spirit? How she was never really happy, especially with her. All the years Mama stood with her back to them and pretended to wash dishes that had already been washed.

When did she start to get sick, was it when I first left, and no one told me? After what seemed like hours of thinking of questions with no answers, she climbed the stairs and entered Mama's bedroom.

"Hi Mama, how are you feeling?" Bree asked and tried not to have stared at her uncomfortably. She was stunned with a shock that rippled through her body. The mama she remembered from just a few months ago had completely transformed. Once plump and full-figured, she was now a woman half her size. The impeccable beauty of her caramel brown skin was darker and dull. The long black hair that once accented her big eyes had thinned out and was salt and pepper. Bree's eyes became heavy with tears as she stood at the foot of the bed, and watched Mama as she quietly slept. She was no longer the woman Bree once knew, now weakened to the point of needing assistance with appointments and chores around the house.

Bree struggled with how to have expressed her reactions to her mother after so many years of indifferences between them. For a very brief moment, Mama opened her eyes. Without having said a word, Mama told Bree, "Thank you" with her eyes.

Based on the way Mama looked in the bed, Bree knew her brother or father had not at all been equipped to have taken care of her needs. Her brother could not have provided her with the things she needed in order to have been fed and bathed. And as for Daddy the marital vows he took years ago for better or worst clearly meant only when things were better.

The start of summer brought new life to the ranch and improvements to Mama's recovery. She still took long naps and was not eating the portions the doctor had prescribed. But she said she felt better, and she actually looked better. Daily strolls in the gardens were heard as the noisy old wheelchair was pushed along the cobbler stone path. She loved the smell of the roses that had bloomed in May and clung to life until September's end. They stopped, and she watched as Mama absorbed herself into the essence of the smell of the red roses because they gave off the most scent.

Bree had substituted for different teachers at the high school and junior high school in order to have kept busy during the spring months. But as the school year ended, she was left with the task to have taken care of Mama. There were days when she and Mama's relationship seemed to have grown. Yet on other days it seemed to have reverted back to the old days where she felt it was dead. These were the times all the feelings that were suppressed and swept under the rug, resurfaced. These were the times she found a spot on the tire swing and communicated with the universe.

"Why is she still so mean? Why does she have so much anger towards me?" She often cried out with no answers returned. Junior always showed up when he saw his sister on the swing. By summer's end, Bree had grown weary.

"Are you all right? You need anything?" This was Junior's code to have given her what she needed to have kept her head above the water she felt like she was drowning in.

Autumn arrived with fall's majestic simplicity, as the first leaves decorated the forest and fields that surrounded the grounds of the house. Bree was ready for the yellows, reds, oranges, and golds to comfort her soul with their warm energy. Her tolerance had worn to the size of a single strand of thread, and she felt like she had dug herself back into a hole.

Then she watched fall as it drifted into yet another season of winter. Mama's health had gotten remarkably better. She was back in the kitchen at her favorite spot in front of the window. The old dirty yellow and white curtains were taken down and replaced with Christmas curtains that had pretty red Poinsettias. Bree and Mama had worked together and organized the house for Christmas, and the highly anticipated visits from Aunt Mamie and Cousin Matthew. Although not completely back to herself, they drove around town and ran errands. Mama frolicked around the house, and complained about every detail Bree had decorated in the house. From the lights that surrounded the front door to the silver garlands Bree had hung on the massive Christmas tree in the foyer.

"No, put the red ornaments around the middle, and the silver ones at the bottom. They will look better than the gold ones you got on there now. Take those off," Mama demanded.

Well, at least she's not in too darker place today, thanks to the Universe. Bree welcomed this side, if only for temporarily.

Bree and Mama pushed through and finished the last of the Christmas decorations.

"We better get ready to go pick up Mamie, Bree."

"Yes, Mama."

They walked to the top of the stairs, and glared back down at the beauty they had created. Smiles and warmth were felt. Outfits were quickly changed from the labors of the day.

"Mama are you ready?" Bree shouted from the kitchen.

"I'm right here. Stop all that screaming."

Excitement filled the car for the ride to the Amtrax Train Station in Yemassee, South Carolina.

Bree and Mama arrived at the train station an hour earlier than the train's arrival time in order to have avoided the hectic rush during that particular time of the year. They were both reeled with joy to pickup Aunt Mamie. Aunt Mamie had taken the twelve-hour train ride from New York because she was not a fan of flying.

"I wouldn't be caught dead on one of those planes." Aunt Mamie would say. "They ain't safe. Always dropping out the sky like dead flies."

Aunt Mamie came down the narrow steps of the train's carriage with a smile brighter than the lights on the Christmas tree Bree had spent hours and decorated to Mama's specifications.

"Hey, Berta!! How are you feeling, sis? Aunt Mamie grabbed Mama with both hands.

"You are looking a lot better than the last time I saw you." Aunt Mamie's excitement was loud as she gave Mama a kiss.

Since her sickness, things were not as festive, and breezy between Mama and her sister. Mama constantly complained. When Aunt Mamie changed the subject, Mama became irritated.

"I'm getting better, through the grace of God and prayers from Reverend Phillips, sis. How about you, Mamie? How was that long ride?" Mama's face became serene when Aunt Mamie wrapped her arms around her and gave her a kiss.

"Where is my little Bree, Bree," Aunt Mamie asked, playing their usual game of 'I see you' that they played when she was younger.

"Here I am, Aunt Mamie," Bree said with excitement as she ran from behind Mama. Aunt Mamie grabbed her favorite niece and gave her a great big old bear hug and a kiss on each jaw.

Junior had unwillingly gone to the airport for Cousin Matthew. He took the bribe money Mama gave him and added what he needed for his supply stash down by the pond. He had a little hide away with a trap door only he and his white friends knew about. He had accidentally mentioned it one day when he had drank too much one afternoon by the swing.

They arrived back at the house within minutes of each other. Aunt Mamie opened the front door of the car before it had come to a stop. She jumped from the front seat and ran like a track athlete full steam to Cousin Matthew and Junior. She grabbed them both at the same time and planted big kisses on their faces. Aunt Mamie always brought a refreshing element of zen and balance to the house.

For the next two weeks, the house was filled with cooking competitions between Mama and Aunt Mamie. They competed for bragging rights on who had made the best tasting meal. The house buzzed with visits from other family members. And trips to the massive garden to pick and gather healthy home-grown greens. Lots of tasty and savory meats baked, fried, stewed, and grilled.

Aunt Sarah was talked about on occasions whenever the conversations transitioned to the past. Bree wondered who she was, since she had never met her aunt. She passed away during the birth of her child and they always talked in codes about her death. Bree never understood why.

This was the perfect time for the house to have gained some sense of normalcy. After all, Bree had returned to the house at such an inopportune time and life had been so chaotic. Aunt Mamie and Cousin Matthew brought the happiness and love to the house that Bree needed the most. For two weeks, the house was filled with feelings of joy, and felt more like a home than the cold and dry house she was accustomed to.

But the two-week visit came to an end way too soon. It was now just a memory as they sat and waited at the Amtrax Train Station for Aunt Mamie's return train with bitter sweet smiles. Bree's sense of stability sank to the bottom of her stomach. She felt the stream of tears that flowed down her cheeks like a river. Cousin Matthew had left the day after Christmas because he had to work. Bree's mood was low as she said farewell to her only true and real connection to family.

The visit brought out a different side of Mama, a more loving and gentler side. Although, the treasured existence of this side had only lasted for a brief moment.

After Aunt Mamie's visit, she and Mama called each other on Sunday afternoons. Bree was called to the phone, and was only allowed to have said a quick 'hello.' But it was not the same as the warm, cozy, fuzzy feelings she had felt when her animated aunt and favorite cousin were at the house.

Bree saw how the bouts with Mama's sickness had taken a toll. Not only had it made a difference in her physical appearance, but she also suffered mentally

and emotionally. She complained more and was not as engaged in the way she once cooked. The taste of her dishes became harder and harder to have digested because they lacked proper preparation and seasonings. She went back to a time when she gossiped.

The holidays ended with a bang for Bree, but the bang fizzled when Daddy snapped her back to reality.

"Gal, you been around here for a while now, and well, you are going to need to find some work. I know you are taking care of your Mama, but you need to find something to do."

"Yes, sir, and just what do you suggest I do here in Sticksville with a degree in art, sir?" She snapped with sarcasm. "First of all..." she started and then stopped.

"Well, I'm going to need some help with the books and answering the phone when we are out in the fields," Daddy said.

"Your brother ain't been too much help lately. That boy has been more pain than gain." Daddy went on about Junior's worthlessness, but eventually remembered that Bree was in the room.

Somewhere deep down in the pits of his mean-spirited soul, he decided that Bree was the only choice he had to have maintained the business's secrecy and to not have questioned him about the books. Not to have mentioned the money for college, he felt she owed him. He decided to have given her the responsibility to work the books and the administrative side of things, like answering the phone.

Stuck, caring for a woman that didn't care for her, in a one-horse town that offered no opportunities, Bree was tired. The hole she was in grew deeper and narrower, and she felt panic as it sat in. She took several deep breaths to have calmed the energy around herself.

The once clear skies that hovered above turned quickly to dark and dreary rain clouds in her mind, with no sign or sight of hope or stars beyond the clouds worth reaching for.

BRIGHTER DAYS WILL COME AFTER PAIN RAINS DOWN

A cold and misty morning took a turn for the worst after Bree drove Mama to her appointment at Dr. Yusef's office.

"Mrs. Breeze, how are you doing today?" Dr. Yusef asked with a thick Middle- Eastern accent.

"I'm doing fair. Still having those pains in my back, and my appetite is not like it used to be. That child cooks, but when it gets done, I don't want to eat."

"Well, the reason for that is because of what we found out after running several blood tests. The results came back, and you have a rare form of a kidney disease, Mrs. Breeze. It is something you have had all your life. You were born with it.

"Kidney problems, what is that?" Mama looked completely baffled.

"You have a form of what is called Polycystic Kidney Disease or PKD as it is called in the medical world. The disease causes many symptoms, such as the ones you have described, Roberta. Over the years, your kidneys have developed fluid-filled cysts. These cysts over the years have changed the shape of your kidneys and made them much larger. Does anyone in your family have problems with their kidneys?" "No, not that I know of. My sister Sarah died young, but I'm not sure from what, or what was wrong with her."

247

"This disease developed from your father. Your father would have been the carrier, Roberta. Do you understand?"

"I have never heard of this before."

Bree looked on as the conversation continued.

"Well, Roberta, with that being said, we are going to have to start you on treatments that will help to eliminate the fluid that builds up in your body because your kidneys do not get rid of it. Your body then builds up with poisons and toxins because the kidneys would have filtered these impurities from your body. Now this will require you to travel to the Dialysis Clinic in Columbia, which is an hour away from your home."

"Lord have mercy. When do I start?"

"Your first visit is 5:30, Monday morning.

"Yes sir," Mama said, though she looked even more baffled than when she had first arrived.

Bree had not thought of Grandpa Monroe for years since he was never talked about.

She replayed Dr. Yusef's conversation in her mind in order to have made sense of it. Mama has a kidney disease called Polycystic Kidney Disease. And it's led to her kidney failure, so she will be placed on dialysis three times a week.

"Mama, when did Grandpa Monroe die?"

"Uh, what child? What did you say?"

"Grandpa Monroe, when did he die?"

"A long time ago, he died when I was a baby. I don't know much more than that. Nobody really talked much about him, especially your Grandma." Mama's face became sad, and the conversation ended. On the ride home, the only sound in the car was the gospel that played on the radio.

After a night of tossing and turning Bree and Mama struggled to have prepared for the long day ahead. Bree pushed herself out of bed and headed to the shower. She dressed and maneuvered down the stairs. Mama sat at the kitchen table and sipped from her piping hot cup of coffee. Bree grabbed a cup from the cabinet and poured herself a cup as well. Mama took her last sip, and stood up ready to go.

"Are you ready, Mama? Bree asked with a yawn.

It was still dark outside when they made their way to the car at 4:00 am. The first day of Mama's treatment Bree endured the long one-hour, mind-numbing drive to the dialysis center. She drove with extra caution, monitoring and following the speed limits. The ride was briefly conversation less, and Bree liked it better that way. But just as she became comfortable with only the sounds of the radio, Mama turned in her direction and started a conversation about the latest, frivolous gossip.

249

Something passed on from her best friend, Mazzella. Mazzella was said to have carried the entire town's dirty laundry. She called the house every day and shared the heartbeat of what had happened throughout the entire Allendale County.

"Not today, I really am not in the mood for this;" Bree slurred the words at Mama. She would have much preferred the sound of silence rather than to have heard about this nonsense.

"Child did you hear about what killed Mary?" Mama blurted-out from out of nowhere, a statement that had nothing to do with anything.

"No ma'am, how did she die?"

"She was sitting around that house worrying about that old no good for nothing boy of hers, and she had a heart attack. She worried so much about Jimmy, with his old sorry behind. He could've done more to have helped his mama out after his daddy died. Just lazy and crazy. He never did finish school you know. But he's done now. Yeah, old Jimmy- Boy ain't got anybody to take care of him, now."

The conversation went on and on for the entire time of the trip.

Bree's life became a living and breathing nightmare of long rides with thoughtless conversations, long stays in hospital waiting rooms, and ambulance rides with tears in her eyes from the uncertainty of doctor's diagnoses. Three days a week for fifteen years of her life was spent transporting Mama back and forth to dialysis treatments. She spent more days and nights than she could have counted in various hospitals. Nights on hospital chairs and couches to have caught a few hours of needed sleep. She was the sole caretaker for Mama, with occasional relief from her Aunt Mamie.

"Mama, you know the doctor said for you not to eat all that fried food. I should probably bake the chicken instead," Bree reminded Mama as she stood at the sink and cleaned the chicken pieces.

"Fry that chicken child, that doctor crazier than you, both of you." Her words came from a nasty place.

"He told you with your condition, baked would be better, didn't he?" Bree asked Mama from an even nastier place.

God knows I'm trying with this old woman, and she is just as tough as a bag of nails. She is about to push me over the edge, done got on my last nerve, damn.

Bree washed the dishes and wiped down the counters near the stove. The phone rang and startled her. Mama jumped and shouted at Bree to get the phone.

"Good evening, this is Dr. Yusef's assistant. May I please speak to Mrs. Roberta Breeze?" The voice on the other end of the phone questioned with politeness.

251

"Yes, hold on, please." Bree then handed Mama the phone. Mama, snatched the phone.

"Yes, sir, we'll be there. Thank-you. Good-bye." Silence briefly, then, "Bree, Bree come here, child."

"I'm right here."

"We need to go to the hospital in Charleston. He said the Medical College Hospital. They found a match for me to get another kidney. Go down there to the office and tell your Daddy. We have to go now."

For the first time since she had been diagnosed with what was said to be a terminal disease, she saw hope in Mama's face.

"Yes, Mama," Bree's voice faded into the air as she ran through the backdoor.

Bree's tiny little feet moved her quickly across the grass of the backyard to the office that sat at the end of the path behind the house. He was not alone. The shiny new car that the light skinned lady drove sat near the gardens. Daddy jumped from his chair when she opened the door. The stranger that had frequent the front of the house, but never came to the door was within Bree's reach.

"What do you want, gal?" Daddy said with his usual viciousness.

"Mama has got to get to the hospital in Charleston, tonight; they found a kidney for her. She told me to come tell you." She said out of breath and looked in the direction of the stranger.

"Go and get Junior. He can drive yawl. I got things here that I have got to get done."

His eyes escorted Bree out the door.

"Wow, you are such a nasty, no, I mean disgusting old man. I hate you." Bree's mind thought what her mouth did not say.

Bree found Junior, and he drove them to the hospital in silence. The drive took them over and hour. Then they waited in the lobby for Dr. Yusef to have arrived.

"Roberta, we found a match," Dr. Yusef excitedly announced. This time with less of his strong accent.

"Your mama's match was a success. She's resting now. You can go in when she wakes up. But Roberta is going to need to get plenty of rest when she gets back home. Do you understand?"

"Yes, doctor. Thank-you. Thank you very much, Dr. Yusef," Bree said as Junior looked on.

"I'll be back tomorrow. You can stay here tonight." Junior said to Bree as he made his way out of Mama's room. He left and headed back for the hour and a half long ride to the house.

Bree looked out the hospital's window into the night

with thoughts of how the actions of today would have change Mama's life for tomorrow. Night fell upon the day, and Bree collapsed and cuddled up in the recliner near Mama's bed. She heard Mama's mumbled words as the anesthesia began to have worn off beneath the pain medications.

"Bree, Bree, where are you? Bree?"

"Go back to sleep Mama. You need your rest."

Mama continued to have searched the room for Bree's presence. Bree moved to the edge of her seat and listened with intensity in order to have understood Mama's inaudible words.

"Bree, I'm sorry, so sorry. I have not been a good mama to you. I'm sorry about."

"Sorry about what, Mama?" Bree asked just as the nurse walked in with another round of pain medication. What was she talking about, what did she mean?

Thoughts of what Mama was sorry for made it impossible for Bree to have fallen asleep. She tossed and turned from side to side bewildered by Mama's words. After an hour or more of the struggle, sleep won. But she was unsure if she was asleep or awake when she heard a voice very clear in the room.

"Bree, where are you? Bree, Bree?"

Bree wiggled and wiggled, but the more she moved,

the more it seemed that she was in quick sand. She felt as if her nose was the only thing visible. The voice called again.

"Bree, where are you? Bree, Bree, Bree?"

Bree's body was frozen and unable to have shaken loose from the clutches of what held her down. The voice trailed in and out, and Bree answered yes to each question. In its last attempt to have reached her, the voice explained why she had been summoned.

After the episode in the hospital room, she realized Mama had carried the heavy burdens of others all her life.

On that unpredictable night she discovered that it had taken this life-changing event to have unmasked Mama's deepest inner feelings. The fifteen years of bumpy disagreeable, and on some occasions enjoyable rides three days a week from the house to the clinic, with the woman she thought she knew.

The transplant for Mama brought about new meanings for life for both of them. They had received a second chance. Bree's returned flight back to the coop was now shining with hope.

HATE OVER LOVE

"Let no man pull you low enough to hate him." – Martin Luther King

Six years today, I have been in this hell hole." Bree frowned at the phone that never stopped ringing. She found herself in an agitated state as she marked the sixth year working in the confinement of Daddy's office. Bree had experienced all his despicable and abnormal behavior firsthand with constant flair up's and toe to toe blows with Junior.

It was a hot afternoon, Junior had been working in the fields since he had left the house after breakfast. He walked into the office and told Daddy about a problem with the equipment not working. He had been drinking and the smell of gin was in the air.

"What do you want now boy?" Daddy barked.

"We've run into a problem when we tried to have loaded that last truck. They put too much on it, and well it broke the axle." Junior tried to explain but the gin had created a problem with his explanation.

"Boy you should know by now how much is enough on those loads. You can be so stupid sometimes. Let me take that back, all the time."

Junior eyed Daddy as he sat behind the desk, with a look of disgust.

 "Look, old man, I'm getting tired of you calling me

stupid. Keep on with that old mouth of yours. One of these days I'll knock the dust off you. Always talking loud and saying nothing."

Junior said through the thick smell of gin that had covered the office.

"Boy, you had better go ahead back out there and fix that truck, before I knock you through that door. With your crazy self."

"Just try it, old man. I'll slap you so hard that when you quit rolling, them old clothes you got on will be out of style." Junior slurred his words.

Bree turned a deaf ear as the threats went on until Junior had slammed the door. Visits from the lady that drove the new cars and wore the fancy suits came more often. She was only known as Ms. Sophie. Once Bree started working in the office, Ms. Sophie and Daddy found a new place to have their rendezvouses.

"Who is that woman?" Bree asked Daddy one afternoon as she looked out the window at the shiny new car.

"Mine your business, and stay out of mine. Stay in your lane, girl. Go ahead back to the house, that's enough for today," Daddy said with his normal cruel tone.

"Whatever old man, I don't even know why Mama stay with your old trifling behind. You ain't right!"

she screamed and walked out the same door Junior had slammed.

Ms. Sophie sat in her car, and avoided eye contact with Bree. Bree rolled her eyes in the direction of the car.

Mama's health had improved after the kidney transplant, and it gave her a new zest for life. And somewhat of a different attitude towards Bree.

Mama was out in the rose garden when the phone rang. She had started working on bringing the garden back to life. She walked to the foyer and answered the phone that sat on the round table.

"Hello Mrs. Breeze, how are you feeling today?"

"I'm doing good? Who is this?"

"It's Cheryl, Bree's friend from high school."

"May I please speak to Bree?" An excited voice asked from the other end of the receiver.

"Oh, hold on."

"Bree, Bree, come and get the phone. Your friend Cheryl wants to talk to you." Mama shouted not knowing where Bree was.

"I got it," Bree said, drained after the incident with Daddy. She had walked by Mama in the garden and sat in the kitchen.

259

"Well, hello stranger, long time no hear from," Cheryl said to Bree and giggled.

"Hey girlfriend! Oh my goodness, how are you?" Bree asked as her spirit now perked up.

"Well, Bree, as you probably have heard, Michael and I, you remember Michael, right? We are getting married, and I want you to be my maid of honor. Please, please, don't say no."

"Yes! Of course I will, "Bree said with excitement.

Cheryl's phone call got Bree to thinking about her own life and the fact that she had not been in any type of relationship. There were a couple of dates here and there in college, minus weird Kenneth. But she had not realized until now that she had nothing or anyone to have shown for her romantic life.

The few times she embarked on dating, ended with dreadful disappointments. She was always reminded of the words Mama and Daddy kept alive about boys.

 "Child, if you mess around them old hard head boys, you are going to end up with a child on your hip. You will not bring a child in this house."

She was told these types of distorted things over and over. It held her back. That and the fact that she never saw any examples of great relationships, other than her friends' parents.

Her parent's union epitomized the picture of what a

dysfunctional marriage was. When her parents should have instilled the values of a healthy male and female relationship, they instead introduced her to a distorted and melancholy point of view. Bree was consistently told to not look at, touch, or talk to boys because it led to some how a child that would have ended up on her hip.

The scary imagery of a child being on her hip was etched in her mind, and caused her to have avoided the dating scene like the bubonic plague.

Love was foreign to Bree. She had no idea what so ever how to have been in a relationship, or how to have shown love. She felt in her heart that love was for the foolish and faint at heart. It made you weak when you opened your heart, and your inner being would just be hurt and torn apart. And that honestly scared her.

"I will not let anything, or anyone control me like Mama lets Daddy," she pledged to herself. Giving her heart to someone meant she risked losing her self, whether by a little or a lot. This frightened her, and she felt ill-equipped to have handled it. Avoiding romance looked a whole lot more enticing for the taste.

Bree's face was lit with excitement as she dressed for her high school friends, Cheryl and Michael's wedding. Her maid of honor's dress was a perfect fit after hours and hours of complaining with the seamstress that had sewed each stitch.

"Mama I'm leaving now. Bree said as she walked past her in the kitchen.

"That sure is a pretty dress. You could have done something else with your hair, though."

"Bye Mama." Bree refused to have let Mama gotten under her skin.

She arrived at the church and the entire parking lot was filled with guests and well wishes that filed into the church. An opened spot near the back entrance, Bree parked and walked to the side door as she lifted her dress from the ground.

"Hi Bree!" The entire bridal party said giggling like they were back in high school.

"Everybody look so good. Where's the bride to be?" Bree asked and looked around for Cheryl.

Cheryl walked from behind the petitioned wall that concealed her from the others.

"Wow! You look amazing. Bree said to Cheryl and walked over and gently gave her a quick hug.

The wedding planner knocked gently on the door and entered.

"Cheryl, sweetie it's time. Are you ladies ready?

"Yes, yes we are. The giggling party moved into the

hall and were escorted to the front of the church. Bree walked with Cheryl. Michael stood proudly at the front of the church, and his eyes searched only to see his soon to be wife. Each of the ten bridesmaids grabbed the arm of their assigned groomsmen and walked to the beat of Stevie Wonder's A Ribbon in the Sky. Bree and Sammy were the last to have entered and the backdoors were closed.

Cheryl's niece entered and dropped rose petals on the white runner that covered the red carpet. With a stroke of the piano's key, the music changed to The First Time Ever I Saw Your Face and Cheryl slowly strolled down the aisle escorted by her father. The entire church congregation stood to their feet, and ewed and oweed at how stunning Cheryl looked. Michael's eyes lit up as he moved to escort his wife to be to the alter.

"Not yet son." Pastor Jones said and pulled Michael back.

The congregation burst into laughter. Michael stepped back into his place by Sammy, but kept his eyes glued on Cheryl.

"Michael and Cheryl's wedding was like a fairy tale," Bree said to Sammy as they sat and caught up on old times.

"Yes, old high school sweethearts, that finally jumped the broom," Sammy chuckled and winked his right eye at Bree. "What about you, Bree, Bree?

When are you going down the aisle and jumping the broom?" Sammy asked.

"What about you, Mr. Single Sammy?" Bree questioned her lifelong partner in crime.

"Nah, not yet, having too much fun, my friend," Sammy said with a smile that seemed to have hid his true sentiments. He worked at Allendale-Fairfax High School as a physical education teacher and the head basketball coach.

"Okay, Coach, just asking, just asking," Bree said as she looked at her friend in a different way.

Then it was time for Cheryl to have tossed her white and teal bouquet, made up of fresh peonies, tulips, ranunculus, and protea into the air for all the single females at the wedding.

"Calling all single ladies," a chubby dj with the sultry voice announced. Playfully and full of giggles, six eligible bridesmaids made their way to the center of the floor.

"One, two, three, here it goes!" Cheryl said as she turned her back and tossed the arrangement high into the air. It was as if it was destined to be because the floral masterpiece landed in Bree's hands. She looked like a baby deer that had wandered away from her mother.

"You're next my friend," Cheryl said as she hugged her best friend and maid of honor.

"Now it's time for all the fellows who are still free. Come on down!" The articulate and well-dressed wedding planner, Mrs. Mays, said in an excited voice. She flagged the guys to the center of the floor. There was a lot more males than females. Bree observed the bunch with curiosity and a hint of pleasure. Sammy strolled to the center after the others. Michael reached and removed the white garter from his now wife's right thigh.

"Oh, careful young man," Cheryl's father said out loud from the table where the bride and groom's parents sat. Laughter and giggles covered the reception hall.

"Ready? Here it is!!" Michael tossed the garter behind his back and looked over his right shoulder. "All right my brother," Michael said to Sammy as the garter rested around his left thumb.

"Wow, ladies and gentlemen, we have our next couple folks," Mrs. Mays said in Bree and Sammy's direction.

Sammy winked at Bree and extended his hand in her direction for a dance. She heard the words of her favorite slow song and hurried towards her friend.

"Heatwave, that's my song," she said as she belted the words in Sammy's ears. "Always and forever. Each moment with you is just like a dream to me; that somehow came true, and I know tomorrow will still be the same. Cause we've got a life of love that

265

won't ever change."

The day ended and Bree left the wedding with mixed thoughts and sensations. She rode back in silence focused on how beautiful the day had been. Feelings started to have surfaced about Sammy and how much she enjoyed him. She arrived at home and the house was completely dark. Thrilled no one was up, she quietly removed her shoes and walked slowly to her bedroom. She stood in the window and looked out at the stillness of the night. Thoughts covered her mind of when Daddy said no one would ever marry her because of how she looked. Tears welled in her eyes, because she felt maybe he was right.

Mama's health suffered complications from the transplant. Bree once again was driving her to dialysis three times a week.

Her milestone birthday in August brought a new set of problems and awkward conversations from her father. She hung the phone up and saw Daddy's shadow hovering in the doorway.

"I need to talk to you when you get done with that."

"Uh-huh, what do you want?"

Her soul dropped whenever Daddy said; "I need to talk to you."

"I might as well get this mess over," Bree said to herself.

"What do you want to talk about?" Bree stood in the door that led into Daddy's office.

"Well, you know you're not getting any younger, and you need to start thinking about getting married. You know a woman is like a rose. One day what looks good is going to fade and dry up."

"What in the world are you talking about?"

He made constant reminders that the time on her clock was running out. Made the whole marriage thing seem a lot easier said than done. In a place where the pickings were slim to none and no prospects were brought home after four and a half years of college. Bree's skin crawled every time the statement was said.

"Really, old man, who are you to give me or anybody else advice about marriage? Do you remember the words you crammed in my ears and down my throat all those years? Do you know how hurtful those words were, do you? Do you?" She screamed at Daddy as her body quivered from past pain. "You said marriage was impossible for someone as dark and ugly as me. Do you not remember your nasty, nasty words?"

Without another word Daddy slithered off like the snake he was, and turned the back of his chair to Bree's face. Bree ended her day on her own. She grabbed the keys to her little green Volkswagen Beetle and slammed the office door. The engine

267

started and a trail of dust was left in the driveway. Headed in no particular direction or specific place, Bree felt her pulse as it had started to race like the engine of the car.

Her spontanious journey ended in front of the recently built fitness center on Main Street amongst the other new business ventures. Not sure why she was there, she parked anyway.

Bree needed another set of ears, but more importantly a strong bear hug like the ones her Grandma Lilly used to give. Since her grandmother had transitioned from her earthly place she missed her gentleness and sweetness..

She sat silently in her car confronting her uninterrupted thoughts about relationships. With no foundation of how to have built a relationship worthy of marriage. A sensitive basket case completely ill-equipped, and without answers on how to have loved someone or how to be loved back. The universe was not in her favor. In a place where she was vastly confused, Bree tried to have convinced herself that just maybe, maybe Daddy's idea about her getting married was not too far fetched.

"This could be my ticket away from that God-forsaken place." Craized thoughts ran rampant through her mind although her heart had not agreed. Even if this was to have become a reality, who would it be? The only males she saw were the sleezy characters that dealt with Daddy and Junior.

Sammy saw Bree as she stepped on the sidewalk in front of the fitness center. He had used the money received from a car accident, and built a fitness center at the corner of Main Street. The facility was used for athletes he taught and coached at the high school to have trained and lift weights.

"Hey, Ms. Bree. Where are you going on this beautiful day?" Sammy teased his friend.

"Hey, Mr. Bighead," she said with a sad smile.

"Where are you headed?"

"Nowhere special, just needed a break from them and that place."

"Want to grab a bite to eat? What about if we share our favorite banana split at the drug store? Come on, you can't say no to a banana split with extra cherries, now can you?"

"You think that you are so cool, with your old big head and flat feet? Yeah, think you are cool like the other side of a pillow," Bree said and laughed this time without the pain.

They spent the afternoon going down memory lane. The most beautiful thing they discovered that day was that although they had gone in separate directions, they had not grown apart. Her heart treasured this happy time with her old friend and partner in crime. Sammy was like a charming

269

gardener who had made her soul bloom.

SUNDAY LOVE

Dingy old Reverend Phillips stood in front of the congregation in his black robe with gold trim the Sunday before Valentine's Day. The choirs sang their normal rounds of hymns from the senior choir, and upbeat tempos from the C.C. Phillips Junior Choir. Deacon Mayer's had read his abnormal round of long-winded scriptures and ended the morning devotion with an even longer prayer.

"Amen, and amen, "the small congregation said with relief that old Deacon Mayer's was done. Bree rolled her eyes to the ceiling when she saw Reverend Phillips mosey up to the podium and started his theatrical performance.

"Let the church say amen, amen again and amen one more time, one for the Father, one for the son, and one for the Holy Spirit."

"Look at him, hair fried, dyed and laid to the side. Not a gray hair in sight. Can't tell where the robe stopped and that old ugly face began," Bree said with a smirk out louder than she had intended.

"Shh, ugh, "came from the old lady that sat next to her, and smelled like moth balls. She pulled herself up, straighter in the pew, and away from the unwanted odors that surrounded her pew partner. The church was not as filled as usual. Members were scattered about among the pews that sent the illusion that the church was fuller than it looked.

271

It was a different kind of fourth Sunday sermon than his same old bored messages.

"If you have your bibles, please turn with me to, 1 Corinthians 13:4-5. Amen. Say amen when you find it. The Lord said in this body of scripture: Love is patient, love is kind. It does not envy. It does not boast; it is not proud. It does not dishonor others, it is not self-seeking, it is not easily angered, and it keeps no record of wrongs. I'm going to tag this text; Love, marriage, commitment, and happiness. Can I get an amen?"

At the end of his hour and a half long performance, the deacons assembled behind the tables at the front and collected the fees for God's word. Then Deacon Brown and the others gathered the trays that held the monies, and made their way to the back of the church to have counted or in most cases miscounted the collections. Reverend Phillips made his final appearance of the day at the podium for the prayer and dismissal.

"Brothers and sisters, before we adjourn and go our separate ways. Today, I want to introduce to the congregation a new member. He is my wife's sister, Dorothy's son. Come on up here, Jonathon, so they can see you, son."

Bree was smitten and started grinning' like a possum eating' a sweet tater. "Lord have mercy, he is fine," Bree said louder than she should have.

Sunday afternoon dinner at the ranch was nicer after

services today because the guest from the pulpit came with his uncle. They entered the house, and the couch beckoned old Pastor Money Bucks to his usual spot until he was called to the formal dining table. Jonathon followed closely behind his uncle and practically fell over when he stopped to have spoken to Mama. Bree's eyes were locked on Jonathon; she looked as if she had been hypnotized.

"Come on in Reverend, and bring that boy with you," Daddy shouted and grinned. "He sure is a fine-looking boy. Tell me about yourself, son."

"Well, sir, you already know this gentleman is my uncle. I graduated from the University of South Carolina with a degree in Business Finance, and I work for American Trust Bank, a local bank in Columbia. I came for the weekend to visit my Uncle Phillip and Aunt Jennie. I'm thinking about moving here soon, that's why I joined Uncle Phillip's church. By the way, I really like your house, sir it's really nice," Jonathon said as he seemed to have taken in every single detail.

"Son, are you married or got any children somewhere?"

"Oh, no, sir. Single and no children."

Bree's eyes widen, and she let out a small gasp "Uhm."

"Yawl come on to the table, it's time to eat," Mama

said, and interrupted Bree's staring. The table became a mass of sounds when plates and bowls and conversations were passed around after the long, drawn out blessing of the food was done by the guest of honor.

After the meal was finished, Bree and Jonathon went outside to get away from the madness of the house.

"So, Ms. Bree, what do you like to do, for fun that is?"

"Not a whole lot here to do in Sticksville. Just work for Daddy, take care of my Mama. I paint a lot and write poetry when I have spare time.

"Nice, very nice," Jonathon said and smiled a sneaky smile.

Bree remembered a wise saying from a psychology course she had taken her junior year. The saying said, "Don't base your decisions on the advice of those who don't have to deal with the results."

At the ripe old age of twenty-seven, Bree was pushed into a very brief courtship with Jonathon by Daddy and their dear cousin, Pastor Phillips. Before she knew what had hit her, she had received a skimpy marriage proposal after a month of visits to the ranch. Three months later, two strangers that thought they knew each other were off to the chapel of love to have jumped the broom.

"Mr. & Mrs. Wallace Breeze would like to beseech

the honor of your presence at the marriage of their daughter Bree Breeze on May 10th, 1985 to Jonathon Williams Jr., son of Mr. & Mrs. Jonathon Williams Sr."

Such exquisite words that Bree had inscribed on customized invitations that were made and mailed to over a thousand guest and family members.

"Today, I have chosen to create a new life with Jonathon, my soon to be lifelong lover and friend. Today I have chosen to embrace joy, happiness, and will put away my negativity and pain," Bree cited the affirmation in front of the mirror she had looked in so many times before. Today she saw an exquisitly good-looking soul that glowed back.

It was wedding day at the Breeze ranch, and the ranch was busy as everyone swarmed around like bees. Planners and the caterers buzzed from place to place.

Susan was hired as Bree's stylist for her wedding day, a recommendation from her matron of honor, Cheryl.

"Please close your eyes, Bree, I need to put the eye liner around these big beautiful eyes of yours," Susan said with soft gentleness. She adjusted the veil, and finished her perfected day of doing what she does best.

"All done, you look gorgeous. I really like your hair

pulled back like that."

"Me too, Susan. You did an amazing job on my hair."

"Time to get on the road to the church, they are outside with the cars. Man, those are some nice limos," Daddy announced. He stood at the foot of the stairs in the tuxedo he had picked for himself and was protested by his daughter. He decided to wear the same color tux as Jonathon. This was against the etiquette of southern weddings, of course, but did he care? Of course not because the day was about him and his glory.

Mama waited in the den and wore an elegant floor length gown that was selected to have matched the primary shade of yellow Bree had used as her accent color. Junior was nowhere to be found. He hated Jonathon because he reminded him too much of his Daddy and the swindler Reverend Phillips.

All were dressed and ready to have impressed the folks in the small community. Bree, and her wedding planner had worked endlessly for weeks after the date was set. Jonathon was her knight that shined in armor. He had come to this place to save her, and they would ride away on his stallion. The meticulous details came together, and resembled a fairy tale storybook wedding. Embedded with so much southern style and charm that it would have made good ole Rhett Butler stopped and stared.

A wedding day designed to be played out like a Cinderella story. All the planner had missed was the horse-drawn pumpkin carriage. But the stretch limos' entrance were a great replacement.

As the wedding cavalcade drove out of the driveway, Daddy struck up one of his weirder than usual conversations.

"Gal, you know this boy is going to make a good husband. He got a lot of good stuff going in his favor. He'll make you a good husband. Reverend Philips said he's a decent boy, and he comes with the highest of praises. We talked about this, and we decided he was good for you."

"What?" Bree turned and snapped at Daddy.

"What are you talking about? What do you mean, you two decided? This is stupid. I don't want to hear your old tired mouth right now." Bree tuned her Daddy out.

The driver stared at them in the rear-view mirror as the conversation trailed off. Bree tried to have placed the ridiculous words and Daddy in the back of her mind and focused on the day in front of her. But his words sparked a place in her heart, and she felt deep down inside that something was not quite right. Something was not right about how this day had come about so quickly.

This was a perfect opportunity to have done what her heartfelt, and the universe had declared before her. But instead her universal thoughts were blocked, and replaced with cardinal cravings of the man that had said he loved and needed her. And over a thousand guests and a bridal party big enough to have filled the entire front section of the church. Not to have mentioned all the preparations and money that had been shelled out.

All the stoppers were pulled out for this fine and fancy day. The stretched Rolls Royce limousine for Bree and Jonathon and three more stretched limousines for her bridal party of twenty plus participants. Her designer wedding gown had a train that covered the entire back of the limo's plush leather seat in a white Rolls Royce with a white chauffeur at the helm.

Fake conversations were passed back and forth between Daddy and the driver with uncomfortable laughter. The driver drove the speed limit to the church. Bree refocused her mind and practiced the vows she had written months earlier, or more so copied from some other sucker, that had saved her the trouble of writing her own. A quick and final rehearsed moment of the vows on the wrinkled paper as they drove into the parking lot of the church.

Large crowds had gathered throughout the church's enormous parking lot. But this took a back seat as she noticed how Daddy's mannerism shifted from one of solicitude to one of complete inattentiveness toward her as the limo parked in the middle of the madness. It was as if a curtain had been lifted, and it was time for him to have given his best performance ever.

After all, he had shelled out a boatload of money for this flamboyant festival.

The universe showed her not only on this day but two months prior that the marriage was doomed from the start. Two months after she had received her engagement ring, she woke up early one morning, and the ring was gone. She had placed the ring in its original box and stored it on the table next to her bed. The room looked like a tornado had hit after she tore the room to pieces when she searched for it.

"Oh my God, where is it, where is my ring?" Bree screamed and felt her chest as it tightened. She immediately ran to her brother's room, but he was nowhere to be found. The need for money for drugs and alcohol had led Junior down a path of, by whatever means necessary to have supplied his needs. He had been caught with stolen items of the family before. But it appeared Bree had become his newest victim.

Bree stomped down to the pond and found Junior. He sat on an old wooden crate and sipped from his cup.

"Junior, where is my ring? I know you got it, where is my cotton picking ring?" She was out of breath and furious.

"What are you talking about? I don't know what the heck you are talking about. Get out of my face with all this crazy mess." Junior said and slurred his words.

279

Bree realized she was not getting any place with him. She turned and headed back to the house. The phone rang just as she opened the backdoor.

"Hello, this is Butler's Pawn Shop," an elderly voice said from the other end of the phone.

"Yes, how can I help you?" Bree asked.

"We have some items, including a ring that maybe yawls stuff."

"Really, how do you know it's our stuff?"

"The fellow that brought it in told the police it was yawls, after he was arrested."

Daddy drove to the pawn shop and retrieved the items that had gone missing from the house. He knew this had Junior's signature written all over it, but he refused to have confronted him or to have pressed criminal charges.

"Gal, put this ring somewhere safe, so that old roguish brother of yours can't get it again."

She wondered why she felt this was a message from the universe, an omen.

Bree's entrance into the foyer of the church was met with Mama's penetrating eyes from one of the stools that decorated the outer area of the church. The hairs on the back of her neck stood up from Mama's look and the thickness of the air. An unsettling thickness.

Reverend Phillips opened the doors of the main entrance. "What do you want me to tell these people? This is a mess, Wallace."

"Tell them about what?" Daddy snapped at old Reverend Phillips.

Cheryl ran toward Bree and wrapped her arms firmly around her best friend.

"Bree, I am so sorry, so very sorry," Cheryl said, and gasped for air.

"What's wrong, what's wrong?" Bree looked at Mama, and then at Cheryl.

"What are you all talking about?" Daddy leaped into the conversation before Cheryl could have responded.

"Bree, Jonathon isn't here.

He's not coming, Bree.

I'm so sorry," Cheryl said through thick sobs and flowing tears.

"What is everybody talking about?" Bree looked at Cheryl and then back to her almost future mother-in-law.

"Bree he's gone." Cheryl said and tried to have comforted her friend.

"Cheryl watched her friend, as Bree went completely numb and crumpled to the floor.

Bree was carried into a room off to the side, and away from where eyes that looked down on her. She was placed on the plaid colored couch with her head on a pillow and her feet elevated. Cheryl closed the door and knelt down beside Bree.

"Cheryl I don't understand. What happened? Where's Jonathon? " Bree slowly spoke.

A light knock was heard on the door before Cheryl could have answered.

"May I come in please?" Jonathon's mother peaked her head in, and preceded into the small room.

"Where is Jonathon? Where is he?" Bree repeated.

"Bree I thought for sure he was going to change his mind and come." Jonathon's mother said to Bree.

"Change his mind? Change his mind about what?" Bree said with forcefulness.

" JJ went along with your Daddy and Phillip's plan to marry you. Your Daddy paid him. I'm sorry, Bree. He just didn't love you and decided he couldn't do it. He told me about it, but I thought he was coming after it had gone this far. I didn't think he would not have shown up."

"I'll be, I'll be dam!" Bree's words faded off.

Cheryl stood to her feet and left the room as Bree turned her back to Jonathon's mother. She reentered the church, and walked to the front.

"Family and friends, may I have your attention please, please. Quiet down, quiet down, please," Cheryl said as she stood and tried to have calmed the restless crowd since the wedding was now an hour past due.

"Family and friends, due to an unforeseen circumstance, the wedding is off." The announcement stunned the entire church. Bree heard the words vaguely for the second time over the church's PA system. "The ceremony we gathered here today for was called off by the groom. He left a few minutes ago after his arrival."

"What the hell is going on?

Reverend you said he would do this. I paid him a nice grip, even bought that ring. I look like a real fool." Daddy confronted Reverend Phillips with fire in his eyes. Jonathon was gone. "How could I have been so gullible? All the signs were there." Bree said to Cheryl after she had returned to the small room.

Cheryl and Michael drove Bree back to the house. They rode in silence while Bree sobbed quietly in the back seat. Overwhelmed with confused thoughts about love. Jonathon told her he loved her. He promised her he would have always been there for her, that he was her knight in shining armor. If this

283

was love or a facsimile there of, she no longer wanted any part of it.

At the age of twenty-eight, she thought she had found someone that she was in love with and was in love with her. Someone she thought she would have spent the rest of her life with, have had children with, and relished grandchildren together. Although she didn't have the tiniest clue of what love was. She never dreamt that on her wedding day that her dream would have been deferred.

The evil plan was for Jonathon to have helped Daddy managed the devious acts of the ranch's wheelings and dealings. Jonathon and old good for nothing Reverend Phillips would have gained a sizeable piece of the pie. Reverend Phillips' pockets would have stayed lined with green because he came up with the scheme.

She thought back to the Sunday Jonathon came to dinner with that old despicable uncle of his. How he sold Jonathon to the family and her like a horse on an auctioning block. She cried a prayer to the universe for help.

Not knowing what this thing called love looked or felt like, she found herself on yet another roller coaster ride. Bree decided that she would not give anyone the power to have pulled her low enough to have hated them.

TRUTH NOT TOLD

"I want to talk to you about something, something I should have told you a long time ago." The aura of the room darkened as Mama spoke.

"What is it, Mama, what do you want now?" Bree asked but truly was not in the mood to have heard one of her long-winded gossip stories. She watched Mama as she fidgeted in the seat, and wrung her hands like a wash cloth.

"Bree, I have had to carry this burden with me all of this time. Everyday whenever I looked at you, I knew you weren't my child, but I have had to have raised you like my own.

"What? What are you talking about?" Bree's facial expression spoke loudly with bewilderment. The atmosphere of the room felt gloomy. Mama continued her confession.

"Your real mama was my sister Sarah. She died after she had you.

"My real mama, what are you talking about?" Bree yelled. "Just hear me out before you go getting mad. This is not easy, and I should have told you about this a long time ago. But I just couldn't. Lord knows this has been on my mind every single day of my life.

Bree, the last child I had died right after she was born. I had already lost four babies before her birth. The doctor told me to not try again because something was going on with my kidneys. After Junior was born, I was told not to have any more children. But that wasn't good enough for your Daddy. He just had to have another boy, another son. Lord have mercy the pain I have been through.

When Sarah had you, her labor pains and probably the heaviness in her heart about what she and your Daddy had done was too much for her body to have taken. Bree your Daddy slept with my Sister Sarah. Well, when she passed away right after you were born, we had to have decided where you would go since Sarah was gone. Your Daddy stepped up and said we would bring you here to be raised. This was close to the time I had loss my baby girl. I found out shortly after we brought you home the whole truth about them. Years passed, he thought it was best to not have told anyone, especially you.

'We are going to keep this under my hat,'" he said. Those old big stupid hats he wore around here, looking like a fresh fool that just fell off the back of a turnip truck. He wasn't happy when Sarah had that girl, I mean you. Pitching a fit around here for years, every time he saw you, he got madder and madder. He wasn't happy at all because you weren't that other boy he wanted." Mama continued to speak uninterrupted unloading the family's dirty laundry.

"Wait a minute, you mean, Mat and I are sister and brother?" Bree jumped from the bed like a panther that had stalked and caught its prey. She grabbed

Mama's, frail, and petite body as she told the family's biggest secret.

"Bree, Bree, I did my best to have loved you, but you reminded me too much of Sarah and what she and your Daddy had done behind my back. You are the spitting image of Sarah. You got her body and all that wild hair just like her. I tried to tell you at the hospital because I didn't think I was going to make it like Sarah. But when I got better, I tried to move from all those bitter feelings I had about you because none of this was your fault. Every time you walked in and out this house, I saw both of them in you. The way you talked, laughed, and walked out to that swing, you stayed on to stay away from me. I kept my back turned and looked out that kitchen window for so many years in order to have not dealt with the truth. I am so sorry I treated you the way I did all these years. I saw and felt your pain, but did nothing. I can't tell you how horrible I feel. Bree, if you can find it in your heart, I plead with you to please forgive me for not being a mama to you, a good mama. I have been such a mean and nasty person. You didn't need to be treated like that."

"Why, why, why?" Bree repeated over and over as she ran from her bedroom, and down the stairs.

"Please, forgive me." Mama's voice faded, now fainted in the background.

Bree needed some air to have caught her breath and

to have cleared her mind.

The skeletons from the past ran deeper than she could have possibly ever imagined. Mama's confession brought such great internal suffering. Bree found herself in the tire swing with her back to the house. Her body quivered and shook uncontrollably. After an hour or more, she removed her dazed body off the swing and stormed to Daddy's office. He sat behind the enormous mahogany desk in the matching chair.

"What do you need?" He asked, agitated

"I need to ask you something, right now, and you better answer me with the truth," Bree blurted out without a thought or care of whom else may be in the office.

"Who do you think that you are talking to like that? I don't have time for you and your whining," Daddy belted out.

"I'm talking to you, you no good piece of –" Bree stopped herself. Then continued. "You are going to hear what I have to say. When were you going to tell me who my real mama was? You are a nasty piece of nothing, I wouldn't even wipe my shoes on."

"What? What are you talking about, gal?"

"You know what I'm talking about, don't act stupid," Bree shouted at Daddy.

"You better watch that little smart behind mouth of

yours, gal." Daddy said and jumped to his feet.

"Answer my question," Bree slammed her hands on the desk.

Junior was within ear shot of the conversation on the truck dock. He overheard and watched the entire ordeal without either of them having a clue he was there. Junior was in complete disbelief as he overheard the conversation.

"Man that old man is something else, a sickening low down and dirty piece of crap." Junior said to himself and stormed off the dock. He hopped into his car and drove off like a bat out of hell.

Bree left the office and ran into the house past Mama. She ran upstairs and slammed her bedroom door.

This has got to be the worse day of my entire life Bree was crushed. She sat in a fetal position on the floor of her bedroom as she stewed and sulked over what she had just learned.

"I hate all of them!" Bree screeched.

The information she was told weighed heavily in her heart. A rage of fiery hell welled up in her like nothing she had ever felt before when she pulled herself to her feet.

Junior drove back into the driveway, and she watched him from her bedroom window. She contemplated her next move. Junior walked to his favorite place down by the pond. She stood by the window and felt a chill run through her veins.

"I hate them. I hate them all," she said through her tears.

After his visit to his favorite location, Junior made his way into the kitchen.

"Old woman, I'm hungry. What do you have fixed to eat"? Junior said to Mama.

"I got some greens, and I can put some gravy over some rice. Do you want some of this stew beef?" she said and fixed his plate diligently without waiting for a response. He was just as angry at Mama for the family's secrets as Daddy. After he gobbled up the food with big bites without chewing, he got up from the table where he had sat alone.

"Where is Bree?" He asked Mama heatedly.

"I'm not sure, she might still be upstairs. She was mad when she left out of here. She got the right to be mad," she replied, reeling with hurt as well.

"You got that right. She has the right to be mad at both of yawl. All those lies yawl told her all this time," Junior's eyes gazed at Mama. The chair at the table hit the floor when he kicked it over before he had left the room and the conversation.

Bree entered the kitchen just as the chair hit the floor.

"Are you alright?" Junior asked Bree with a hint of

compassion for the first time in a while. He saw the suffering she felt in her eyes. They stood in the kitchen and stared at the back of Mama's turned back. "I'll get him for this, and all the other things he's done," Junior pledged with sternness.

Bree and Junior left the kitchen and Mama. For the first time in their lives, Bree and her brother sat at the edge of his bed and had a heart to heart talk about the man they agreed was the most despicable man on earth. She shared how she had found out about how Mama was not her Mama.

"So that makes old cousin Mat your brother, huh?" Junior made a point.

"Yeah, I guess so. All this time and I never even knew. I wondered why he felt such an urgent need to protect me."

"I wonder if he knows."

"I don't know. He said one time he did not know how his mom; I mean our Mama died. That Grandma Lilly never really told him anything when he lived with her. I guess Grandma must have been ashamed."

Her mind moved to the idea of Matthew being her brother and not Junior. For a brief and quick moment, she smiled inwardly and the pain subsided. She got up from Junior's bed and moved in the direction of the closed door.

"I luv you sis," Junior said to the only sister he had known all his life.

The view of her brightly lit bedroom was blurred by her tears as she entered, and plopped down into the chair next to the window. Tears streamed as she balled again like a newborn baby. Her soul felt depleted.

You can't go back and change the beginning, but you can start where you are and change the ending.

~C.S. Lewis

"Hello, hello Berta is that you?"

"Yes, its' me Mamie. How are you doing?"

"I am doing good, Mamie. I guess the devil must be working overtime today, I'm sweating like a pig in a pen. It's hot as heck here."

"Mamie I finally had to tell Bree about Sarah being her real mama. It hurt her so bad. Knowing what that thing did, the wounds were freshly re-opened. Mamie I'm so mad all over again. Lord knows if I wasn't a Christian, I'd blow his tail to hell. She deserves better than this, Mamie."

"I agree Berta, they both do and you are way past due in doing something about this. Sis, you should have faced this mess and that monster you got for a husband a long time ago instead of standing there all those years with your back turned in that kitchen.

Yes, Berta there is a time to be silent, and a time to speak up. It's time now for you to stand up. Kick his tail to the curb with both your feet."

"I love you too, sis." Mama said to her sister for the first time in a long time. A firey streak of hell's heat raised up in her, a heat that could only be compared to the heat outside the walls of the house.

Mama sat silently in the kitchen, alone and cried. As she cried, the words of the song she sang in the choir surfaced and filled the hollowness of the house.

"Lord I need your guidance and your strength.

Show me the way, show me the way.

I've been searchin' for a long time

I knew that it was something that that I had to find (I've been searchin')

You should have seen me wringing my hands and crying.

It was all because I couldn't find peace of mind and it was then,

oh I kneeled down to pray I said Lord

Will you show me the way (the way, way).

It was the Canton Spirituals' and the song reminded her that sometimes all it takes is another chance, a second chance to right your wrongs.

"Where are you going?" A voice trailed Mama as she left the kitchen. Her brisk and exaggerated steps brought her face to face with the pretty light skinned lady that drove the new shiny cars. Sophie always sat at the edge of the yard and never came to the door. The battle at that moment in time was not with her, but with the beast that sat inside.

The strong wind that pushed the door opened startled Wallace. Mama stood and faced the man she had hid from over the past three decades.

"What is wrong with you, opening that door like that, woman?" Wallace said with a clenched jaw as he jumped to his feet.

"Sit down! Sit your old tired and trifling behind down before I step around that desk and knock you down."

"Who do you think that you are talking to like that, woman? You must have lost the little bit of sense I thought you had."

"Ain't anybody here but me and you, and that old whore sitting outside. So, you are going to sit your old wrinkled behind down, and shut your pie hole or I'll shut it for you!"

Wallace's body crumpled back into the chair.

"That child in there is hurting, hurting so bad because

I finally told her the truth, the truth about you and Sarah. A secret I have worn around here like nasty dirty laundry, feeling on most days like I was locked up in a casket. But today is the day I freed me. Freed me from this pain and mess you made years ago."

"What are you yacking about woman? What are you saying, flying up in here like you ain't got the sense God gave a goose?"

"I'm going to get all this heaviness off my chest once and for all. Now shut your mouth. You slept with my sister, and yawl had a child I had to raise because you didn't want anything to do with her. Just because she wasn't that precious son you wanted. Never did let me grieve the lost of my baby girl. You just walked out the room that day just like it was any other day of the week.

"You treated Junior like he wasn't apart of this family. But you finally drove him to being just like you. You took his manhood from him when he couldn't go to school no more. I was never a good mama to them, never stood up to you for how you treated them, and I hated myself every time I looked in a mirror. But I despised you and Sarah more, God rest her soul. I watched you treat both of those children like the scum of the earth, and me even worse. You paid that no count boy to marry that child, and he ran off like the coward he was. But he was smart, smart enough to have seen you for the worthless piece of nothing you are. That thing hurt

295

me so bad. I wanted her to get married and have some happiness, and to get away from here and you. You have done a lot of wrong, and a lot of damage to both of them. My sister too. Lord knows you ain't done right by any of us. I know that you have been fooling around with Ms. Light Skinned that has sat out there all these years. Driving up in this yard, sitting around this office all hours of the night and day, I knew."

"What? Why are you talking like a crazy person?"

"Shut-up, yes, I have been crazy for a long time. Letting you treat me like something less than a doormat. But today, Mr. High and Mighty your time is up. I want you and that old jezebel that's been sitting around this place all these years to get off this property. I'm going to take this land and make it a land of promise for me, Bree, and Junior. Something you should have done for your family."

"Woman you need to go back to the house. You should be thanking me for all I have done for yawl. Go away from here with all that foolish talking. I ain't got time for this mess today or no other day. Go back to the house and mind your business. All I did for yawl, you got the nerve to come in here and spit in my face, you unappreciative woman. Get out of my face."

"I am, but when you get back to the house, it won't be the same."

Mama once again walked past the car Sophie sat in. This time she walked over and hit the hood of the car with both fists.

"Bree, where is Junior?"

"He's in his room, why?"

"I need yawl to come down here."

Bree and Junior obeyed Mama and made their way down the stairs and sat in their assigned seats at the kitchen table. Today Mama faced them and her back faced the window.

"Look, I know our last conversation didn't go well, and the two of you are hurting from these things that should have been said years ago. I should have done more to have protected both of you from the horrors of this house, and your Daddy. Yes, he has been a good provider of things and stuff for us to look good to the outside world. But on the inside of these walls, it's been just like a volcano waiting to explode. He was never able to give us the one thing we needed the most, the ability to have shown how to have loved each other."

"What are you talking about?" Junior's impatience got the best of him, and he lashed out at Mama.

"Yea, what are you talking about?" Bree chimed in.

"Just be patient, please. I have got to get the weight of these burdens off my heart, so my soul can be at ease. " Mama said and recited the same speech she had said to her husband less than an hour before.

297

"But now Lord. We are going to take this ranch from that monster out there and make it a land we can be proud of and pass it on to other generations beyond yawl."

"What?" Bree and Junior's looks at Mama spoke volumes beyond the perplexed thoughts that danced in their heads.

"All that stuff that's been growing in those backfields is over. We are going to nurture this earth and these fields with goodness and purity. Crops will be grown to help and not harm people. Do yawl understand? We are good people, and we need to do good for others."

Bree and Junior looked at each other but never spoke a word.

"With that being said, there are some things the three of us will need to do. I need you two to understand this is going to make our lives better because that big, bad black monster will be gone."

Summer had placed a miserable heat on the night. It was a hot and humid night filled with a heavy sense of unpredictability. After the conversation between Bree's Mama and Daddy, Daddy tucked himself neatly away in his office.

Junior left after the conversation with Mama and Bree. He returned as the heat of the day had dissipated, and it was now pitch black dark. He parked outside the office. He had travelled to

Bushfield Airport in Augusta, Georgia, and picked up the guest of honor for their evening meeting. His return to the office was the signal Bree and Mama used to move to their positions. The anxiety of the crew was kicked into high gear.

Bree's mind drifted quickly back to the occasional times when Junior had tried to have protected her from Daddy's wrath. The times she saw the brokenness of Mama's spirit in her face when she looked through the kitchen's window from the porch. The hurt that had festered in her heart, the harbored anger, and the raw hate that ran hot and cold at the same time.

Bree's "Birdwild" spirit was freed from secrets of the past she had felt for so many years. Birdwild's freedom fueled the energy Bree needed to have helped Junior and Mama to have carried out their plan for a future with greener grass.

"Look at him."

She observed the stillness of Daddy's dark silhouette behind the half drawn black out curtains in his office. The mid July night was only lit with fireflies, and the faint light from the office. Humidity hung in the night air so thick it could have been cut with a butter knife.

"I guess there were times when he did some good."Bree comtiplated in her mind.

Her mind flashed back to earlier days when Daddy

had shown those moments of being semi-decent to her and Junior.

Well, he provided us with the comforts of worldly luxuries, paid my way completely through four and a half years of college, and gave me a place and position in the family business after I flew back to the coop to take care of Mama. He may not have been the best at how to have loved us, but he was a soldier when it came to being a provider.

Bree's mind raced with so many thoughts that tugged at her heart.

"Are you all ready?" Mama looked at Bree and Junior. They both nodded their heads and gave a slight smile.

"What about you, young man?"

"Yes ma'am, ready whenever you give me my signal." His smile in the dark revealed almost perfectly white teeth.

Junior entered the dimly lit office that was occupied by Daddy and the light skinned lady that always seem to be somewhere near. Tonight she seemed to have blended in very well with the trash can she sat behind.

"Hem, Hem." They both jumped like startled rabbits when Junior cleared his throat.

"What the hell?!" Daddy shouted in Junior's

direction. "What are you doing here, boy?" He was totally pissed off because his head still buzzed with anger from the earlier conversation with Mama. Bree entered into the cluttered office after Junior.

"What do you want, gal?" The question was pelted in Bree's direction with a rage greater than minutes before.

"Well, I guess you are about to find out, huh?" Junior said. Mama walked into the mix, unannounced. The office space became even more congested when a man none of them had ever seen before, even Daddy, entered.

"Who is this man with you, Berta?" Daddy asked as all eyes turned towards the stranger.

"This is Daniel, Wallace. Daniel meet Wallace." Mama made the formal introductions.

"Good evening, sir." Daniel said with politeness and a smile. "Who is this man, Berta?"

"I just told you his name. This is Daniel. He's a lawyer from Greenville, Wallace. He's here because he has some papers for you to sign."

"Papers, papers for what? What is this craziness yawl talking about, bringing this stranger in here at this hour of the night?"

"Well, ever since Deacon Benjamin came to see me on that faithful day after my transplant, my life has

301

never been the same since. His visit, unlike the visits you never made, told me of just how low down and dirty you are. He shared with me a secret you don't even know. Lord knows I tried to have forgiven you for all the other things you have done in the past. But when Deacon found out about Daniel, and what he knew about you and his wife, what's her name?

"Sophie."

"That's right, Sophie Benjamin. I'm sorry, I meant, Robinson. You changed it back to your maiden name when Deacon threw you out, right? Ya'll never really legally divorced, did you? Mama looked at Sophie.

"Deacon Benjamin told me all about that jezebel that's been keeping you company all hours of the day and night. I guess she never told you they were married years ago and he threw her out. You sitting up in church Sunday after Sunday grinning in Deacon Benjamin's face, and didn't even know that you were messing around with his wife." Mama said with a look that looked like she had bitten into a raw onion.

Wallace looked at Sophie with eyes that seemed to be the size of two half dollars.

"But that's not all. Daniel's got something else to tell you, some icing for the cake." Mama chimed back in.

"Yes, I most certainly do, sir. Well, when I turned sixteen, something didn't seem right about the family I was with. I didn't seem to fit in anymore.

Something was missing; the dots never seemed to have flowed to the right place to have been connected. So, I asked my mother one day the question no mother wants to hear. Are you my real mother? My father was sitting across the table from me as we ate dinner. A very nice and cozy dinner I might add. My father answered instead of my mother. He said it was time. Time I knew the truth because everyone is entitled to know the truth about who they are whether it's good or bad. A wise philosopher, Aristotle, once said, 'Knowing yourself is the beginning of all wisdom.' I found out on that day, two days after my sixteenth birthday I had been adopted."

"Adopted? What does this have to do with any of this?" Daddy barked.

"Well, Wallace it has everything to do with all of this. "Wallace I remember so well that night I heard you and her out here in this yard arguing and fighting, blowing up a storm. And then she stopped coming around here for a while. You remember, right? She got in that brand-new car you had just bought her, and high tailed it out the front gates like a witch on a broom. But I know she still kept in touch because the phone calls started to come, and you and her would carry on, on that phone day after day. Guess that was her way of hiding this boy right here from you. She had him and didn't want nothing to do with him. Just gave him to her brother and sister-in-law. They took him with them while they travelled

303

with the Air Force. Yeah, Lord knows they did a hell of a better job than the two of you would have ever done with this boy. So see Wallace, you have another son. She didn't tell you that, did she? Isn't that something? Look at him Wallace, such a handsome smart and successful young man." Mama finished and watched Daddy's face as it went blank.

Junior frowned.

Daddy's mouth moved but no words escaped. Bree saw for the first time a look of shocked fear as tears welled up in his eyes. Sophie's eyes moved from her lover to her son. A son she had never seen or touched since he had left her womb.

The laundry hanging out to dry on the line in front of him was heavy with the dirty water it had soaked in all those years. Confessions had flowed faster than the currents in the Savannah River.

Daddy looked at his second son dressed in a black three-piece pinstriped suit. He stood humbly, and spoke articulately to his audience in the room.

"Mrs. Roberta reached out to me through Deacon Benjamin awhile back, and we started the wheels to turning. Now, if we can get down to why we are here. Enough of this sentimental trip down memory lane, don't you agree mommy dearest?" Daniel said to the woman who had given him life.

Daddy tried to have spoken, but still nothing came out. He looked as if someone had hit his mute button.

"Mr. Breeze, these are papers Mrs. Roberta asked me to have drawn up. This is your copy. Mrs. Roberta, you already have yours."

"Boy what the hell is this about? What are these papers for?"

"Well, Mrs. Roberta wants you off this property, or she is willing to testify in court about the illegal dealings you have been doing. She's got enough proof and evidence from Junior and the books Bree have kept to put you behind bars for the rest of your little pitiful life."

"What in the world?"

"Mr. Breeze, you will need to sign here, and intial in the places where it asks you to initial. The actions of the papers are effective immediately."

Junior and Bree looked at each other, and then focused their attention on Daddy. They saw his expressionless face. A blank slate.

"The last page is your divorce decree, sir. I will need your signature there as well."

BRIDGE TO PEACEFUL WATERS

Bree reminisced about her wedding fiasco and thoughts came to mind about her disenchanted life.

"Will my life rise above the storms I have been through, and will I find sunshine?"

"Am I going to grow old in this place, with no one to ever have shared my life with?" Bree said with tears in her eyes as she looked at her reflection in the floor length mirror in her bedroom.

Most of her life had been filled with stormy rain. She desired to find a rainbow. Because they had always appeared at the end of summer storms, and brought splendor and tranquility to her spirit.

She learned that as much as she would have liked to, she could not have wiped the slate clean, or erased her past or reversed her mistakes. Because what was done was done and no, the bell could not have been un-rung."

She had detached some of the emotional baggage she had carried since the night in the overcrowded office. When the pressure cooker's top blew off, the family's enigmas were brought out of darkness and into the light.

"Child you have to turn the other cheek, kiss and make up." She remembered Grandma Lilly would always say.

She knew beyond a shadow of a doubt she had to give that second chance she would have wanted others to have given to her. Her pain, however, made it hard for her sometimes to have opened any doors to others for the fear of hurt all over again. As an adult, she too often wondered why with all her hurt she should have to give so much energy to others. Bree recognized that at the age of twenty-nine she had lost so much time by not letting go. She also recognized that when she stubbornly refused to have passed on second chances, her life suffered more than others.

Life did not suddenly become a bed of roses, but she made great strides and progressed beyond her pain. There were still zigs and zags, hiccups, and turns that pushed and pulled her like the sails of a sailboat in the wind, but she held tight to her boat's stern. The animosity she harbored toward Mama, Junior, and Daddy although he was no longer at the house was relinquished. Doing so released strongholds that had bonded her to the past.

She made a decision and took her second chance, her "second take." A new beginning made a world of difference in her life and the lives of the aunt she once knew as her Mama and the second brother she gained.

As the spiritual leader, Pir Vilayat once said, "Every moment is the chance of a lifetime."

In other words, every moment was a new beginning.

Bree relished every second of her second chance that Mother Earth had provided her. It was up to her as she breathed each new breath to have relinquished the old and embraced that second chance to have made changes.

A second chance was how she moved forward and gained a normalized life. A moment gone by in the blinked of an eye was a moment gone, never to be returned.

"God puts rainbows in the clouds so that each of us in the dreariest and most dreaded moments can see a possibility of hope." Maya Angelou

"You ready, big-head?" Matthew asked his sister with a smile bigger than the ocean in front of them. Bree was captivated by the majestic beauty and grace that the waves of the turquoise ocean brought as each flowed in and back out. She felt in her spirit that the ocean at that moment swept away years of pain, as it pounded against the golden sand. Such a majestic mystery that took Bree's breath away.

Her heart pounded as she stood on the pier and waited for her cue to have moved to the bottom. Her heart knew that the man that waited at the bottom of the bridge was not perfect, but he was perfect for her. She believed they were mere drops of dew separately, but together they would have the same power of the ocean they stood before.

Tears of joy this time streamed down her face.

309

Matthew nudged his sister's arm.

"Ah, don't start that. You old big water bag," Matthew teased her, in an attempted way to have alleviated her anxiety.

"All the pain that you have been through is now behind you. Look at all you have in front of you, what you've gained," Matthew encouraged her, and wrapped his big arms around his sister, and pulled her into his broad chest.

"You are so right Mat. You have been so good to me all my life. The brother I wanted but never knew all along I had. Thank you, big brother for always loving me and making me laugh when the world seemed so cruel and mean. Because of you, yes, I'm ready," Bree smiled and kissed Mat on the cheek.

They moved onto the wooden and tattered steps that led to the ocean. Junior waited at the bottom of the stairs.

"Are you ready, my ole big-headed sister?" Junior smiled at his cousin, and Bree kissed him on the jaw.

"Yes, I'm ready! Readier than ever," Bree said as Junior and Matthew took each of her arms, and led her to the life she deserved. Before she reached the end of the aisle covered in yellow rose petals, Sammy met his friend and escorted her the remainder of the way, and her two brothers trailed proudly behind. Sammy reached and took Bree's hand. He leaned to have kissed her face through the veil, and their eyes locked as if they had seen each other for the very first time. "Not yet, man," Matthew teased his soon to be brother-in-law.

"Alright bros," Sammy said and air-punched towards both his brother-in-law's.

Bree and Sammy stood in silence after they had reached the arch that formed a halo over their heads. Today the universe had answered Bree's calls and opened its blessings to her. The man that had been a part of her life all her life was now devoting his life to her for the rest of their lives.

 On the 24th day of March on the first Saturday after Spring had begun, Bree and the man of her dreams stared into each other's eyes and poured out their hearts to each other at sunrise before some of Mother Earth's greatest wonders. Dolphins danced in the background as the sky pulled back its majestic curtain, and the sun opened like an orange rose. Waves raced with each other to have reached the shore. Their love was agape love because it was selfless, sacrificial, and unconditional that had grown from the time they had gotten into trouble at Sammy's parents' house. Their friendship had weathered the test of time and developed into a profound love of trust, and respect. She had found a man that loved her flaws and all. He looked beyond her battle wounds of life and saw the beauty of her soul.

"I would like to present to some and introduce to others, Mr. and Mrs. Johnson," Minister Fillmore proudly said to the crowd of well-wishers. The new couple turned and faced the crowd. Sammy planted another kiss on his new wife's face. She turned and smiled a grander smile and winked at her new husband. "May I please have your attention, ladies, and gentleman, please? Just for a brief moment," Bree asked the crowd as the waves made it difficult to have been heard. She walked over to where Mama sat near the aisle with the trodden yellow rose petals. Bree took her hands as she knelt in front of her.

"Awhile back, Mama, you told me about my real mother, and it hurt me so very very much. On that day, you asked me if I would forgive you, and I stormed away in anger. I never answered you. Today I need you to know the answer to your question is YES! Yes, Mama I forgive you. I know you aren't my real Mama, but you are the only Mama I have ever known. Through the good and the bad, when I got mad or sad, you were still there as best you could have been. I love you." Bree said to Mama as tears ruined the remainder of her made-up face. Bree stopped questioning why things were the way they were in her past. It was time to have enjoyed the ride in front of her. Sammy and Bree, with their families, stayed on the beach for a private ceremony. They poured sand from the vials they were each given and released their past pains to the ocean's floor as the tides moved the golden sand to its rightful place.

"What the universe will manifest when you are in

alignment with it is a lot more interesting than what you try to manifest."

~ Adyashanti

ACKNOWLEDGEMENT

The process of turning *Birdwild* into a book is truly one of the most internally gratifying experiences of my life. My belief is that anyone who achieves a once in a lifetime goal must acknowledge those that helped, with heartfelt gratitude.

I especially want to thank a remarkable tribe that helped make this a reality.

First and foremost, I give thanks to God for planting the seeds that blossomed into my gift of writing. I thank Him for giving me the wisdom to believe in my passion and to pursue my dreams.

To my husband, Thomas Simmons, whom I am so thankful that you are my husband and in my corner. Thank you for keeping me grounded and pointing out what is really important in life. Thanks for your inspiration, support and not just believing but knowing that I could do this. "I love you."

Patricia Johnson-Childers, a sweet soul whose positive energy encouraged, and moved, me beyond every query letter that came back. I am grateful for your personal reading and honest feedback. Although we have never met face to face, our souls connected through Bree.

Thank you Tahara Saron and the BlackGold Publishing Family where "Literature is Golden" for reading my manuscript and giving me the opportunity to bring my book and characters to life. My gratitude knows no bounds.

Noelle Brooks, the best editing Queen in the world, you are awesome! You taught me how to transition my book, and bring it to fruition. I thank you from the bottom of my heart.

Dwayne Jenkins, for your insight when answering all my millions of questions, and completing the final edits. I really appreciate your timeliness.

Thank you.

Made in the USA
Columbia, SC
03 July 2022

62745946R00176